SPAWN OF SAX

Spawn of Sax

YULE TIDINGS

Lukas Allen

Contents

Prologue   2

Part 1: Luxuria   5

1   6

2   8

3   13

4   20

5   27

6   33

Part 2: Ira   35

7   36

8   40

9   45

10   53

11   58

12	63
13	70

Part 3: Acedia   **75**

14	76
15	81
16	86
17	93
18	99

Part 4: Invidia   **105**

19	106
20	112
21	117
22	123
23	128

Part 5: Avaritia   **133**

24	134
25	137
26	142
27	149

Part 6: Superbia   **155**

28	156
29	163
30	169
31	173

Part 7: Gula   **179**

32	180
33	185
Epilogue	194

For Dad

Prologue

Life continued for me, as an incognito angel on Earth. I got married to Max pretty quickly. We were very lovey dovey for a while, but enjoyed being so even though some people couldn't stomach our sappiness.

Like Nevaeh, my housemate and friend, would say, "Goddamnit, Yule, I'd prefer you and Max lustfully doing it on the table to you rubbing each other's noses and calling each other a sweeter sweetie pie over and over. It would make my stomach churn less."

But her boyfriend, Felix, after Nevaeh left the room in disgust, would wink at me and say, "I think it's cute."

We were happy, in this big house, all together. Max's sister, Fate, and her boyfriend, Maximus, (no relation between Max and Maximus, they just have strangely similar names) were talking about moving to the big city so Maximus could follow his career in football better.

We played football together in our off times, after Max, Nevaeh, and Fate taught us how to play the game. Felix, Maximus, and I didn't know the exact rules as we *used* to all be dead and from times way past, but we enjoyed the physical parts of the game and warmed up to it quickly. I suppose when you used to be gladiators like us three some things will stick with you no matter what.

Like my cat. He stuck with me no matter what… even though I lost track of how old he should be. He looked healthy enough, so I guess it didn't matter.

I continued to help people in any way I could. I lived up to being a true angel on Earth.

I just went to a baptism of my friend's, Tanya's, baby, . It was a shame that the child was brought about because of Tanya's rape in the workplace... but I hoped the kid, Paul, would have a long and healthy life.

She cried over and over at the meetings I made for people like her, for people like Fate, Nevaeh, and I as well. We all had been through that pain of being taken advantage of.

I continued my life, even through the pain and suffering. Being alive again is such a pain in the ass sometimes!

I held the little Paul after Tanya showed him to me.

I looked into his eyes... He looked like a normal human baby. I smiled to myself at that.

Such purity... Such innocence. I never wanted to see that taken from him.

Even though I knew that true evil used to stalk the Earth, that it still does in ways I can't even fathom. I hoped that it would never harm Paul.

True evil... like the Devil, like demons from Hell...

But, the Devil was thrown to the farthest reaches of space by one of his own minions. The Devil was betrayed and defeated by a demon, a demon who now goes by King of Hell.

Hmm... I suppose that's good enough... but I hope the Devil stayed out there for a long, long time... I hope he never claws his way back to Earth.

I hoped this, and I prayed this as well.

I gave Paul back to Tanya. She never wanted to let him go, and smiled at him with such utter love, no matter how he was conceived. It didn't matter, she was his mother.

Paul grew up, and we *each* continued our own lives.

This is the story of how a demon got to the gates of Heaven.

Part 1: Luxuria

Lust

1

"You never cried so much as when you were baptized… but after it was done, you just seemed so happy, like God was smiling through you." my mom said to me, showing me the baby pictures of my baptism.

"Why do we have to be baptized, anyway?" I asked her.

"To wash away our original sin. Humanity disobeyed God, and we carry original sin until we are baptized."

"But doesn't God let us make our own choices? Isn't that why we have free will on Earth?"

"It's not that simple, Paul. We made the choice to disobey God, and it will forever haunt our footsteps until we are baptized and join his church."

"But if God knew we were going to disobey him… why did he let us? Shouldn't he have made us idiots that just obeyed his every command?"

"…I think you're getting far too clever for your age. I think I'll invite Yule over and you can ask her. She knows all about God, and would be an angel if she wasn't alive and breathing."

"Do we have to? She always hugs and kisses me until *I* can't breathe…"

"Yes. Her and her husband, Max, are some of our best friends. I hear your father just come home, will you go meet him? He'd like to see your smiling face. Get your sister, too."

"Alright…" I said, and yelled at my bratty older sister, Dana, that Dad was home.

"Really??" Dana said, "I thought he had a double shift tonight! I'm so happy he's here!"

We went downstairs, and my dad hugged and kissed us, happy to see his children again.

Even though I wasn't his real child. I mean… no one knew but me… I think… but those dreams I had… of *someone else…* being my father. I mean, hell, me and Dad didn't even look alike, and I only had my mother's nose. *I* noticed it… but he still hugged me, even rubbing noses in an Eskimo kiss, since I didn't really like it when he kissed me…

I still loved him though. He was always working, trying to pay for his two kids, and my mom had to quit her job to raise me and Dana. It was great when my dad had off days and me and Dana could just play baseball with him.

I also loved when he swore. He swore like a real man, cussing like the Devil, but always tried to hide it around me and Dana. But still, if he was working on fixing something, he swore like he could care less if God was watching him.

He tucked us into bed, kissed us goodnight as our mom did too, and wound up a music box so I could fall asleep. I heard it plinking out its notes as the light from the hallway shined into my room… and I fell asleep.

I dreamed that I was the son of the King of Hell, but the King of Hell wasn't my dad.

I woke up in a fright. The King of Hell was rather nice, but he seemed to really like jazz, heavy metal, the blues… and biscottis.

I let the dream pass… and fell asleep again, but with a dream of Yule guiding me to Heaven… She was very pretty… and I almost did like her kisses…

2

Yule and Max came to visit us on the weekend after we had all gone to church. We'd always see Yule and Max there, and always talked to them briefly outside after the ceremony had ended.

"Tanya!" Yule said as she entered the house and hugging my mother, "How are things? You barely ever go to our meetings anymore! I know it's kind of pointless now... but it's still nice for you to hang out with us gals."

My mother held Yule's hand and said, "I've just been busy at the house. I had to paint the whole porch the other couple of days, and these two always need a fresh meal... Dang kids. Do they ever stop eating?"

Yule laughed, and said, "Only when they're adults. We've even found a man to join us! He felt a little bit emasculated with us girls, but he quickly saw we weren't so bad, and was soon laughing and crying with the whole lot. It really happens to everyone."

"What kind of club is it?" I asked.

"Adult stuff." my mother said, "Do you need to ask Yule any questions? I'm sure she'd be able to answer them better than me."

I really didn't want to ask this weird, religious, tattooed, albino lady any questions, but I did wonder about something the serpent had said, so I said sure and she took me to the couch.

Max was palling around with my dad, and as I looked at them I realized the question I really wanted to ask. Fuck, this women wanted to answer my questions, then she should answer my real question.

"I'm not my dad's son, am I." I said.

Yule turned a bit paler than she already was, and said, "We're all the sons and daughters of the Lord…"

My mother was distracted with my dad and Max as Max played with Dana, so I continued, "That club… You made it for something horrible that people went through? Why else would they be crying at it? Why did my mom go to it?"

"I believe she'll tell you when you're older. Some things people don't want to do, but still have to do anyway. Your mother and I went through this experience." Yule said.

"So… like rape?" I said.

"…Yes. Some people are forced down a road they can't get out of… Some people are stuck on that path, until someone helps them. I hope I have helped your mother." Yule said.

"So… I am the son of a rapist…" I said, looking down at my feet.

"No, Paul. You are your dad's son. Kasey loves you, and you love him. That is worth more than any sort of forced action." Yule said, "You will always be loved and cherished by your parents, and by God, and me. We all love you, Paul."

"But- But- I- I must be the son of the Devil…" I said.

Yule smiled knowingly, and said, "No. The Devil is gone. You are the son of Kasey. Always remember that."

Max wanted to show us this one magic trick he was practicing. Yule kissed me on the cheek, and I blushed as she did.

Max lost the ace, but I still wondered how the rest of the cards weren't fucked up. He wasn't really a very good magician… but he enjoyed his little party trick.

I pulled the ace out of his sleeve, and Max said, "...Huh. So that's where that went! You could be a practitioner of the dark arts all on yourself, Paul!"

I smiled, even though I was sure that was Max's plan all along, to get me to pull the ace, and I accepted Yule, Max, and my family's applause.

Over the next few days, I practiced that magic trick, over and over.

Gosh, it'd sure be easier if I could just do real magic...

But I eventually got it down to a point, and wondered if I could show my crush this trick...

Do girls even like magic tricks?? I didn't really know. Yule did, but she was Yule... and Tricia... she... might *hate* magic tricks...

I still nervously put the cards in my pocket, and got ready for school. I showed her the trick, after walking up to her gaggle of friends, and she pulled the ace out of my pocket. I said Max's line, and they all giggled. I wondered if I said it right. I nervously walked away, allowing Tricia to keep the ace.

I just sat on my lonesome... No one really liked me here... I wondered if that had anything to do with it being a domineering Catholic school... with our crappy uniforms and crap. Every day we all wore the same thing, if in slightly different colors, beige or blue pants, green, yellow, or red collared shirts... I think if I went to Hell, it would be exactly like Catholic school.

Some bullies picked on me, but I always said snide and sharp comments back to them... They laughed and called me "the comeback kid." I think they picked on me more just for that sharp response... but I had to do something. I couldn't just let them pick on my mother like that.

I really, truly, hated them all.

And strangely, I felt like someone else felt my pain. Maybe Jesus? Maybe he hated the bullies just as much as me. But still... it felt like someone was whispering to me in the crowded crowds of the cafeteria... telling me not to give up.

I was about to walk back home alone... with Dana talking to her friends and being cherished... then Tricia stopped me and said, "I thought you were just being moronic... but then I wondered how you let me take out the ace. Like that was your plan all along."

Even though Max had told me how he did the trick, I smiled and said, "A magician never reveals his secrets."

"Ok... Just know, I thought it was pretty neat. Call me sometime! I'd be interested in what other 'secrets' you can tell me..." she said, and wrote her number down on the ace and handed it to me. I blushed and said sure.

I called her up every night, even though she didn't answer some nights, and we talked. We talked, laughed, and exchanged... secrets.

Then she told the secrets to everyone the next day.

I sat red faced in the cafeteria, as she told people that I got a hard on for an old lady... Yule...

I never said that!! I just said she was pretty!! She went on telling stories about me and Yule... and I hated Tricia as much as the rest. I felt ashamed, embarrassed, and just wanted to walk out those doors and never come back...

I sat outside after school, just depressed as shit, and someone said I could probably use a smoke.

I looked up at him. He looked extremely handsome, but extremely ugly as well. Like Heaven had seemed to frown on such perfection, and wished everyone to know. He was so handsome it was ugly.

He offered me a cigarette, and sat beside me. He said, "Girls are cruel. You were crying because of a girl, weren't you?"

I wiped off my tears, and said, "N-No. I-I... just thought she was different..." and took the cigarette from his hand.

He put one in his mouth and said, "You'll make them love you one way or another. They won't know what they're missing..." and lit the cigarette with a flame coming from his finger.

"H-How did you do that?" I asked.

"Magic. Here, let me help you..." he said, and lit my cigarette for me with his flame. I smoked the cigarette, coughing a bunch. I offered to pay the man for the cigarette, but he said, "It's my treat. It's always good to help a lost soul like me... I believe that you'll do great things one day. Have fun, kid, and remember... *People lust for what they have lost...*" and the man left.

3

I bought a pack of cigarettes from some older kids and smoked when I didn't think anyone was watching. It was harsh, and I didn't really feel happier when smoking, so I wondered why people did. I did feel just a bit relaxed, as the nicotine made my brain feel like it was buzzing.

And I looked so cool! I felt like a gangster from one of those old movies, with a cigarette on my lips. I practiced smoking tricks, exhaling it out my mouth and then inhaling into my nose, pushing the smoke out with my tongue in a heavy cloud, and even tried a smoke ring. I couldn't really get the rings to come out right.

When I was in that secluded lot that no one seemed to go to but me, some bullies from my school rode in with their bikes. "Hey, it's the lost sheep, Paul. Don't you know smoking is baaaaad?" they said, making bleating noises like a sheep at me. They were the most stuffed up, pretentious, elitist bastards, even using their religion education to single out other kids and make themselves feel holier than thou.

"You gonna cry again, Paul? You gonna kill yourself? I truly pity your soul." a bully said.

The tall one got off his bike, and said, "Hey, you should really give me those cigarettes, Paul. I wouldn't want you to catch lung cancer... Give them to me."

"N-No. You just want to smoke them… I've seen you hang out with the older kids, too." I said.

He glared at me with a wicked grin, and said, "You think you hang out with them? You're just an easy mark. I don't think anyone's ever paid thirty dollars for a pack of cigarettes before."

"I-It's illegal for kids, and I just… really needed a smoke…" I said.

They all cackled at me, and he grabbed my shirt collar, and said, "Now give me your cigarettes, sheep boy." I thought about it, was reaching for the cigarettes in my pocket… but he said, "And go crying back to your old lady, too. I'm sure your Yule probably is going to smack your ass cuz you're a bad boy… What? Is she like some 50 year old lady that you hump?"

I got really angry. I pushed him away, and said, "No! She just turned 30 last year, and she's pretty, and nice, and is one of our family's best friends! She could kick all your asses like nothing, too!"

"And she's not here to do that, is she." he said. He pushed me to the ground, but I got up, and whacked him on the cheek with my hand. He doubled back and the bullies all ganged up on me, pushing and grabbing me, hitting me over and over, then took my cigarettes and left, swearing at me.

They left me bleeding on the ground. I sat up, and well… I did get a good whack in. I didn't really have much of a chance, not being the biggest kid on my own and against all of them.

They were cowards in truth, just picking on smaller people, with a big gaggle of them all together. I walked alone, and while it may not have been the safest to do that, at least I didn't need to hide in a crowd.

I walked back home, and Yule was visiting my mother again. They went up to me and asked me what happened. I was bleeding from my nose.

"Nothing… Just had a fight…" I mumbled.

"You've been fighting?? You're going to say sorry to that boy to-morrow, I mean it!" my mom said, wagging a finger at me.

"What, all six of them?" I said.

"Six kids ganged up on you?? Who were they? I'm telling their parents right now!" my mom said.

"No one... I just want to go to my room..." I said.

"What happened, Paul? You can tell us." Yule said.

I sighed angrily, turned to her, and said, "Why are you here, anyway?? Just go to your fairytale world of God and leave me alone!"

"You don't talk to her like that." my mom said.

"It's alright. You don't have to tell me why you got in a fight... But try to make peace with your enemies. I think I'm late for that shopping trip I have planned with Max! He sure does love that place with all their fancy, bizarre clothes. I'm glad it's next to the steak restaurant. We can actually afford the occasional steaks and clothes now! It'll be alright, Paul."

I hugged her, and I was crying as I did. She just kept on hugging me.

In a show of sleight of hand, I pickpocketed her cigarettes out of her pocket.

She waved us goodbye, and my mom set me down in front of the TV.

I just hid the cigarettes in my pocket. Thanks, Yule. This'll make up for you getting me beaten up.

School, and my smoking, continued. It was just run of the mill boring stuff, and I did it alone.

Well, besides Dana... but even though she was nice at times, she was a real brat. She was only older than me by a year, but still acted like she was the boss of me. "Clean up your room, Paul! I have friends coming over!" she yelled at me from outside my door.

"They're not coming into my room, so you and them can deal with it." I said, sitting amongst my mess heap.

"I don't know where you get this nastiness! Look- A bowl of cereal with the milk curdled! I'm going to tell Mom in the garden if you don't clean this up!" Dana said.

I grumbled, kicked the clothes under the bed, and picked up the cereal bowl.

"Thanks, Paul! You look so cuuuute when you're all submissive!" Dana said, laughing. She ran into her room and shut the door before I could catch her and pour the curdled milk on her.

I went walking alone, just into town, and waved my mom goodbye.

It was always nice taking walks. When I used to have a friend we'd just walk around and talk about all sorts of stuff, laughing and making jokes. But he went to a public school… and we just kind of drifted apart. I was thankful that in just a few short years I'd be going to high school… and could choose where I wanted to go.

I asked my mom to let me switch schools, but she and Dad just really wanted me to get a good Catholic education, like my mom had, and let that help me guide my choices later in life. I don't think that they knew that their choice for me was actually driving me away from religion instead of towards it.

Although… my mom says you can always depend on your faith. Even after you think you left it for good, it'll pop up again later in the worst parts of your life, and give you comfort and hope again.

I thought that was bullshit, and honestly thought about worshipping Satan instead.

But Satan wasn't real, just like God… so there would really be no point in worshipping anything.

I saw my one friend, the ugly handsome man with two gorgeous women in his arms. He looked slightly tipsy, but not in a way that would disarm him, no, it just looked like he was more relaxed by letting down his guard for a second under alcohol's influence.

"Hey, kid. What's up? Those bruises make you look pretty wild! Don't they, Georgia? Your husband is a boxer, don't this kid look like he can be a boxer one day?" the man said to the woman in his left arm. She nodded and smiled.

"Hi. Do you have any more cigarettes? My pack ran out pretty quick…" I said.

"Here, kid, take a spare of mine. Remember to savor it! You don't want to end up like Vera's mother and get lung cancer!" he said, throwing me a pack of cigarettes. The woman in his right arm smiled and waved at me.

"Thanks." I said, catching the cigarettes, "I'm Paul."

"Stan. Or you can just call me the Devil. That's what these gals call me in bed!" Stan said and laughed. The women laughed, and Stan said, "You look pretty down on your luck, Paul. Want to come to a cool place with us? A neat little club hidden down below the earth."

"U-Uh… I guess…" I said.

"Then follow us. Be sure to hold Georgia's hand when you cross the street! Don't want you getting hit by a truck." Stan said, and Georgia left Stan's side and held my hand as we walked down the street as I blushed. We went down a back alley and Stan knocked on a big metal door.

They opened up, took one look at him, and let us inside. We walked down the stairs.

There were all sorts of attractive people here… but… there were also things that I've never seen before except in dreams.

Demons.

Georgia led me with Stan. Stan called out to an older blonde woman that looked *very* attractive, and a man with a bull's head. The man with the bull's head mooed to us.

We sat in a booth, and I swore I just saw a demon tail attached to Georgia's ass.

"These costumes are pretty n-neat." I said.

"Oh, yeah, we're a wild bunch down here." Stan said, then shouted out, "A round on me for everyone! Everyone meet Paul, a new member of our family! Cheers, to Paul!"

The demon people cheered for me.

The bartender who had a goat's head put down some beers in front of us, and the rest of them slurped them down. Stan said to me, "Drink up, kid. It'll help dull the pain."

I carefully sipped the beer.

Stan said, as Georgia had her hand on my thigh, "We all are stuck in this place… Forever. This is the closest we'll ever get to Paradise… at the bottom of a bottle. It's always nice seeing a new face… a face like us."

"What do you mean?" I said, and sipped at my beer again.

"Georgia, do the thing, and show him what I mean." Stan said. Georgia turned me towards her, as my heart beat faster and faster, and she kissed me roughly, jamming her tongue… her *forked* tongue, into my mouth.

I looked into her eyes like that, and I thought I saw a vast, cold, pitiless darkness, but worse… were the flames contained in them.

She kept lustfully groping me… and her tail was wrapped around my arm. I could not escape.

She bit my lip, with… fangs.

I liked it, at the start, but it soon felt like she would devour me with her kiss, like she would consume my soul, with her grabbing at my body, putting her hand down my pants and fondling me.

Stan said, "That's enough, Georgia."

Georgia sat back, grinning at me malevolently.

My head felt like it was spinning, and to make it stop… I slurped down the beer.

"Ar-Are you some sort of succubus? A monster?" I said, fearing this woman rubbing her breasts beside me.

Stan said, "I wouldn't call us monsters… just damned souls. *Just like you.*"

I looked into his eyes, and I saw the Prince of Darkness smile at me.

I said I needed to leave, and Stan said, *"You're always welcome in our little slice of Hell."*

I ran out the doors, ran home, and it still felt like that woman was groping me.

4

I tried to wash off the feeling of her touch, but I couldn't get it off. It clung to me, like a permanent mark.

I mean, I was never that aroused before... but also never that frightened. It wasn't a good feeling.

It's like I couldn't do anything in her arms, like I was trapped, and all I could do was accept my fate as she had her way with me.

The thing with her being a demon just scared me all the more. But... I couldn't get her out of my head. Georgia. She was everywhere I looked, in flashes of my eyes when I shut them to go to sleep...

I walked back to the "little slice of Hell."

I was just curious. Maybe she wasn't really a demon? Maybe that was just all the costumes and the shadows in that place? Maybe I could ask her about her and her husband?

The bouncer let me in, grinning a smile with too many teeth, more than what a normal human had and wrongly placed.

I asked the goat headed bartender if Georgia was here.

He led me to a back room with a large mirror in it. Georgia was waiting. She purred, *"I knew you'd come back... Sit beside me. Tell me your secrets..."*

"A-Are you going to blab them all to everyone, if I d-do?" I said, and sat carefully beside her.

"Of course not, sweetie... We're all the same here. We're all alike, man and woman, demon and angel... but we, we need to stick together..." and she stuck her hand on the side of my face, turning me to her, slightly scratching me with her nails.

"Are you really a de-demon? I-I feel like I am the son of the King of Hell. I know, that's stupid... but I think I am not my dad's real son..." I said, and she listened in relish, hearing my darkest thoughts.

"That's because you are the Spawn of Sax, that's right, Sax, the now King of Hell. He did not let us come back... He betrayed us, his kin, and even God has betrayed us forever..."

"G-God? What did he do? He never really did anything, anyway. We're just evolved monkeys, and the whole thing with the story of Genesis is just a story." I said, as she stroked my cheek.

"Exactly my point. God never did anything for us... and we are all damned because of that."

"A-Are you really married to a boxer? That must be a fun life."

"Oh it is... I've never had so much fun dominating and enslaving such a strong man... Humiliating him... torturing him... when he thought he had it all..." she purred, grinning wickedly.

"Y-You're not going to do that to me, are you??"

"Of course not, sweetie. You are the Prince of Hell. A son of the usurper. But you are trapped forever like us. We will make you a King of Earth... But we must wash off the stain of your baptism..."

"Wh-What?"

"Oh... I'm not going to pour baby cow blood on your head or anything... Just bring you into the world of men... You will be a strong man after you are done... Stronger than your human father, and your father in Hell..." she whispered in my ear.

Then she unzipped my pants.

She undid her own and got on top of me.

I was taken by a demon.

I felt like I was taken down to Hell… and well, it did feel kind of nice. Even though she looked like a woman of Hell the whole time, shredded wings, demon tail, cloven hooves, and large horns.

She kissed me on the lips when we were finished, as I shuddered in ecstasy, and she said, *"Welcome to your Hell on Earth. I name you Saul."*

The lights turned on, and I heard laughing, clapping and cheering from behind the mirror.

It was a one way mirror.

Stan walked out with a horde of demons, congratulating me on taking my first real *demonic steps on Earth.*

Georgia cackled as I stared at them all. The blood rushed to my face, and I quickly pulled back up my pants.

I quickly left, embarrassed and ashamed. They had… all watched… they all… saw me… and her…

And Georgia had called me Saul.

What did it mean?? *Was I really a Prince of Hell??*

I couldn't wash off what I had done. I couldn't clean myself, couldn't get her words out of my head.

I thought sex was supposed to be something special?? Something just between two people in love?? I admit, I didn't resist… and it felt so nice…

But I had lost my virginity to a demon. A *married* demon.

I breathed in and out heavily, and just tried to push the thoughts out of my mind.

I couldn't tell my parents, I couldn't tell my sister, I couldn't tell *anyone.* I would have to keep this a secret 'til my grave.

I just took another shower, to wash off the shame.

I felt something sprouting from my rump. I wiggled it back and forth, swished it into my hand… and saw my demon tail.

I screamed.

My mother rushed in as I was in the shower and asked me what was wrong.

"N-Nothing, Mom! Jus-Just nearly slipped!" I stuttered.

"Alright. Be careful, ok?" and she shut the door again.

I got out of the shower and just shoved my new demon tail down the leg of my pants.

This shame was consuming me. I felt like I really was in Hell. And the demon tail meant I belonged there!

But wait! I knew someone I could talk to! If… I couldn't talk to anyone… I could at least talk to Yule. She never blabbed anything I said to her, and she always made me feel… well, loved. Not like a demon succubus. I thought about talking to God, but I thought talking to Yule would be just as good as talking to God, if not better.

I went to Yule's house, telling my mom I just wanted to say hi to her, and knocked on Yule's door.

She opened the door, and bright light seemed to be coming from all around her. I blinked for a second, but I think it was just the lights in her house.

She invited me inside, smiling. I really wanted to talk to her alone, so I'm glad her housemates were all out doing things. I don't know what Yule actually did for work, and she would always be working too, but whenever I needed her she was there, waiting to invite me inside.

Her cat mewled up at me, and I pet him. She sat me on the couch and gave me a soda. "Don't drink too much of that, ok? Won't help you sleep." she said, cracking open her own soda and sitting across from me.

I told her, "I-I… I had sex…"

She nearly let her soda slip from her hand, and said, "Really? …I suppose- you and her probably just felt that attraction, and hormones and instincts, and just couldn't wait… It's nothing to be ashamed of. As long as you used protection. You should probably wait until the time is right, when you feel a little more mature to make such choices. I honestly didn't think you started puberty yet, but just goes to show... you never know!"

"I-I mean... things have been changing for me... B-But... I-I had sex..." I couldn't continue, I couldn't tell her my shame.

"You mentioned that. What is it?" Yule asked.

"I-I... didn't really want to... but... she was so... well, not really pretty, but she was... attractive. An-And... she... undid my pants... and got on me... and- and- they all-" I said, but started crying.

"Oh God..." Yule said, and sat beside me and held my hand as I bawled my eyes out. "Shh... It's ok... Who did this?"

"A lady from the club... Ge-Georgia..." I said.

"Do you mind if I tell your mother? We, together, will make sure she's locked up for this. We'll make sure nothing happens to you again." Yule said, as she held my hand.

"I- No! Please don't tell my mom! She-She'll never understand!" I said.

"Paul... She'll understand more than you think. I understand. It really, truly, is not your fault." Yule said, smiling sadly to me.

"...Alright... Please... can I just stay here for a bit? I-I'm scared what my dad will say t-too... But he'll probably just congratulate me and pat me on the back or something..." I said.

"I doubt that very, very much. Stay as long as you like. I'll let Tanya know you'll be here for awhile, and talk to her in person when I tell her about what happened." Yule said, and left to the kitchen to call my mom.

A Japanese woman walked through the front door, one of Yule's housemates, and a big burly man walked in behind her. The woman, Nevaeh, never went to church, but still was probably Yule's best friend. She said to the big man, "I kinda miss people glaring at me when I was talking to you before, y'know? It was kind of funny having them all think I was nuts."

"It's better this way, I think. I mean, I can't spook anyone like before, but it's a great feeling... being... well, alive again." the big man said.

"Oh! We have company. Heya, chap, what's up?" she said to me.

I had never actually introduced myself to Nevaeh before, but always heard stories about her from Yule. I introduced myself to her, "I'm Saul- I mean... Paul."

"Pleased to meet you. I'm Nevaeh and this is Felix." she said, and they both shook my hand.

I didn't say anything else, and just said one word responses and the like when they asked me questions, so we just watched TV for a bit, while Nevaeh and Felix chatted about their bizarre lives, which they just thought was mundane.

"I'm actually glad you don't have any balls. Can't get me pregnant, and I think you're *really* getting good with- Y'know." Nevaeh said to Felix.

Felix laughed, and said, "It's my pleasure! I never knew you could make such loud- I mean, so you really think we should get that one house?"

"It's time we get out of Yule and Max's hair. Fate and Maximus already moved to the big city, and really are introducing themselves to the world. *Everyone* knows Fate's name since she wrote that big reveal of cults and the like, and Maximus... thinks he can go pro in football soon." Nevaeh said.

"I do miss them. It'll be nice when we can all get together again. The Crusaders of Heaven! I think that should be our team name." Felix said.

Nevaeh laughed, and said, "Sure. It'll be nice having our own place. I realllly like that house. It's sure to be haunted. Maybe we can rustle up some of your friends?"

Felix laughed, and said, "I do hope most have found their way to Paradise."

Yule came back in, and said, "Heya, guys. Are you ready for our meeting? Everyone should be here in an hour."

"Y-Your meeting is happening now??" I said.

"Yup! Feel free to join in or watch if you like. Or you can hang out with Felix. He's practicing some of his old moves he used in the ring, and I'm sure he could teach you." Yule said.

"You were a boxer, Felix?" I asked.

"Well... sort of." Felix said.

"I think... I'd just like to see what that meeting is about, and then learn from Felix. I never want to be put in a situation I can't fight my way out of again." I said.

5

I sat with these gaggle of women in the living room, with Yule, Nevaeh, and one man with pink hair. He looked sad when he looked at me, but like, sad *for* me.

The women all adored me, saying I was the cutest little guy. I really did not want anyone to touch me… and they didn't. But they said stuff like they wanted to, to pinch my cheeks or baby me against their breasts… but they didn't. They respected my space.

They all talked, and right off the bat the man with the pink hair said, "I think I'm ready to talk about it now."

The woman hushed down, and Yule said, "Please do, Benny. We're all here for you."

The women all said the same thing, that they were here for Benny.

He told us all of how he was molested by a man when he was a young teen. He wasn't overly detailed, but… I could truly feel his pain. He finished his sad story, and didn't shed a single tear so far, but after he was done he bawled his eyes out. He told us that when it happened he had just come out as gay, and thought that was what you were supposed to do if you were a homosexual… but the man had taken advantage of him, and it haunted Benny for most of his life.

Yule's group all empathized with him, sympathized with him, and continued their own stories.

I had enough of that, very quickly. I just… felt so sad, even sick to my stomach thinking how something like that could've happened to these people, so I told Yule I was going to go out to the back with Felix.

I watched as he sliced the head off of a homemade practice dummy with only a dagger.

I looked at him wide eyed. He looked like some sort of knife fighter in a back alley, but held himself up like he was the star of an arena, like an old gladiator.

He turned to me, threw the knife up in the air which he caught again and again, and said, "Well. Let's get you out of situations you can only fight out of, shall we?"

"How did you do that?? I didn't think you could cut people's heads off with only a dagger!" I said.

"You probably shouldn't learn how to use a knife yet… Would be dangerous if I gave you a weapon, like the knowledge of fighting with something as dangerous as a knife, and you got into situations that you *can't* fight out of… Would you like to learn some hand to hand techniques? They've saved my life more than once."

"Sure!"

First, Felix just told me how to throw a good punch. Square your feet, snap back, keep your eyes on your target, and if you can, smack 'em in the jaw, as that has the most chance of knocking out your foe.

"We must aim for a quick fight, short, brutal, and polite. You *never* need to taunt your foes, dance back and forth just out of their reach if you can throw a hit. This only serves as entertainment purposes, and really is just a quick fall from grace, as you believe you are raising your pride." Felix said.

"What about when there are a bunch of people after me? Like in a group? What should I do then?" I asked.

"Go for the tallest, biggest guy first. If you can take him down, then the others will see their leader fallen, and at least you won't have to worry about the biggest threat. If there are *swarms and swarms* of them… just try to survive for a little bit longer and things have a chance to come out right. They may get tired, run out of their pawns, and you can eventually catch your second wind and fight back stronger."

"What if I know I can't win?"

"If you are facing insurmountable odds, the best you can do is stall, because you never know who or what has a chance to save your life. If the executioner comes for you, at least ask for a glass of water, and delay it. God could smile on you right before the blade comes down." Felix said, "Didn't happen for me… but, I still tried. And sometimes all we can do is try."

"What is it you exactly mean? You tried?" I asked, and threw a punch in the air.

"…I lost my life before, everything I held dear… But don't worry about it. I eventually got a second chance, and have a new, even better life than I had before." he said.

"Cool." I said, "I'm really so glad that Yule is my family's friend. You guys and her really make me feel… happy."

"We're all here for you, Paul." Felix said.

We went back inside, and the women and Benny were all just joking about things and having fun. When the meeting ended they all hugged each other goodbye, and I shook their hands politely as they left and smiled at me.

Yule rested a hand on my shoulder, and said, "See. You're not alone. A lot of people have been in your shoes, and we, I, care for you."

"Thank you, Yule. I think I'm ready to- Never mind… Can I stay the night? I realize that you're going to have to tell my mother when you see her… and I think I couldn't bear that, at least not until after a good night's sleep…" I said.

"Sure. Feel free to use Fate and Maximus's old room."

"I'd just like to watch TV and fall asleep on the couch, if that's ok."

"Yeah. Bright lights and friendly pictures always help keep the demons in your head back." she said, smiled, and went to get me some blankets.

Demons in my head… I hoped no demons from down the street got in instead.

As I lay snuggled under the blankets watching TV… I felt safe. Like nothing could get into the sanctuary of Yule's house.

In the morning, we went back to my home and Yule told my mother. My mom called me in sick from school, and we just talked. She didn't believe Yule at first, but I told her it was true. My mom went white faced, as I told her all about Georgia and the strange club.

They got the authorities in straight away… but when they went to the club, it looked like it had been abandoned for some time. They gave my mother a fine for wasting police time.

"B-But that's not right!! I-I don't know- I don't understand…" I said. My mother sighed, but said that she believed me, if anything.

Then she went to her room… and I could hear her crying alone.

My dad had already left for work and my sister for school. Yule hugged me anyway, and told me it was alright… but noticed something on my back.

She pulled out the demon tail sticking out of the back of my pants. Her eyes went wide in a fright.

She said, "I-I… I… I need to sort this out… I- Please stay safe, Paul. Just stay safe for now."

She quickly left.

I just sat on the couch.

I thought if Yule had abandoned me... then I was truly abandoned by God.

My family was all worried for me, but they all believed me. I thanked them the most.

Yule... stayed away from me for a while... for a good long while... but eventually when I said I wanted to go to her meetings again, she allowed me to, and I just sat in politeness with the women and Benny.

I told them what happened to me, when I was ready to.

They grew tearful, and one said, "That should've never been... Some men just think something like that is an achievement, a true accomplishment... but you were just taken advantage of. Used. I've been there, when I really thought I was 'just having fun.' And later... as the relationship continued... it showed to be what it really was, just abuse. Nothing special, nothing caring, just using and abusing. You're a strong man, Paul."

They did all call each other "strong women" and I felt strange that they used the phrase on me, as a man, but I did feel just a bit better.

Later, when they had all left, Yule said, "Let's see what we can do about your demon problem..."

"You believe me??" I said.

"Yes. I- I know I should let your mother tell you... but not even your mother knows the whole truth... This- never made any sense..." Yule said, and sighed.

"Then that means... I am a son of the King of Hell??"

"At least you're not the son of Satan... but you remember every story those women told you? That happened to your mother, Tanya, but by a demon from Hell. It's truly horrible to think of... But- I don't understand why they're not all gone..." Yule said.

"C-Can we just cut it off or something??"

"I... I guess? I don't know. Won't that hurt?"

"I do feel pain in it… When I slammed it in the door on accident it hurt like hell."

"Hm. I'd take you to a hospital to remove it… but I just don't think people are ready for a thing like that. Real mortals can't even see demons most of the time, anyway."

"So that means… you're not a real mortal? And I'm a demon??"

"I guess I'm as close to mortal as I'm going to get, these days… But you're not a demon. Maybe half demon? Let's try to remove it." Yule said.

She got Felix and Nevaeh, Max was working late like he did on days with the meeting, and they put my bare ass out on the table. Felix drew his knife and said, "Are you ready?"

I said, "Y-Ye-"

"Already cut it off." Felix said.

I looked back at my ass with the wiggling stump of the tail, and I screamed as blood spurted out.

"Shit." Yule said, and got a towel for me to press against my ass as I continued to scream.

They patched up the stump, and let me sit on the couch and fed me cake that Nevaeh had made.

6

Those bullies were harassing me again after school.

Before they threw their second insult, I whacked the tall guy with my fist, on the chin, knocking him out.

The others backed away.

I told them all to leave me alone.

They did, even though they ran away insulting me.

I sat by the tall guy and smoked, waiting for him to regain consciousness.

He soon did, even though I kind of was afraid I killed him or something, and he said, "Wh-What? Stay back!"

"It's alright. You got what you deserved. Now leave me the fuck alone." I said, flicked my cigarette butt at him, and left.

He chased after me, saying, "H-How did you do that?? I thought you were a wimp! But you knocked me out in one shot!"

"I told you to back off."

So he left, but said, "Hey," and threw me the pack of cigarettes he had stolen from me, not one of them smoked.

He left quickly.

What the fuck??

I thought this kid would hate me forever or something! But instead he throws me back my cigarettes!

He invited me to sit with him at lunch, and some of them were trying to insult me, but he, Renley, told them to back off, and they listened to their ringleader.

I was on my guard the whole lunch, but we actually got along pretty swell. I didn't know this asshole actually had a personality.

Tricia eyed me after that, and tried talking to me again after school.

I turned to her, as she called out to me and waved, and I approached her. I said, "What do you want?"

"I-I just think… how it was cool you took on Renley. I didn't expect you to have a tough side…" she said.

"I fucked a woman in a club."

"…Huh?"

"And she was a demon from Hell, but she was still nicer than you." I said, and walked away.

She burst out crying, but I let her.

Time passed by quickly, and I was soon in high school. I went to a public school, and even though the encounter with Georgia haunted my memories and dreams, I forgot about it for a while for a new exciting life of high school.

The demon tail stayed a stump for now… but I still knew…

That demons were real, somehow on Earth, and I was the son of the King of Hell.

I was Saul and Paul, the Spawn of Sax.

Part 2: Ira

Wrath

7

Renley was on base and I was up to bat.

The pitcher threw a twisty, curvy throw, one I knew he was saving just for me.

I stepped back as he tried to take my head off, and a ball was called.

It was my third ball, and I knew this shithead was just trying to walk me.

On his last one he threw completely away from me, I stepped across the base and I swung.

The ball flew up high, up and up, almost ascending to Heaven, and flew over the fence.

My mom, dad, and Dana were cheering for me as I ran across the bases and got Renley and I home.

We won. I and the team were going to go out for ice cream, but I said my family and I were going out to dinner. It was my parents' anniversary.

I walked to my parents, and saw the ugly handsome man, Stan, watching me from the side with a baseball cap on his head.

He waved at me, started up a cigarette, lighting it with his flame, and walked off.

My heart beat ten times faster when I saw him, but Dana ran up to me hugging me, and said, "You did sooo great! You've really come a long way since when you couldn't even hold a bat right! Good thing Dad taught you everything he knows!"

My dad smiled and hugged me, saying that that homerun was really only something like he's seen when he played baseball in school.

We went out to dinner and had pizza at the Italian restaurant. The owner looked like he shouldn't even be alive anymore, but still clung to that life as he brought out the pizza. He actually looked like he had a bounce in his step, when he should've been walking to his grave.

My parents loved this place. It reminded them of the Italian restaurant they had their first date at in the big city, their hometown.

I always liked that I saw Yule's article of praise for the restaurant, still hanging up on the wall and always cleaned from dust.

The manager called out to the owner, saying, "Marie needs some help with the kids… Tricia is missing again, and the rest of them are sick. I'll see ya later, Dad." and the owner told him good luck.

Tricia?

She had just started dating my best friend, Renley. I always was never super nice to her… but I tolerated her at least. Renley and I got along like nothing else, we did almost everything together, baseball, this really easy class on history that we both joked and laughed at, and just were really great pals. It's a shame I hated him for so long in grade school.

We finished the pizza, and I went to train with Felix. I had sooo many responsibilities in high school… and I was almost certain that as soon as high school was over, these responsibilities would never show their heads again. I did at least an adequate job on them, but still, it was nice having time for what I *really* wanted to do…

I wanted to be a gladiator.

I know, that is the most ridiculous dream anyone's ever said… but Felix told me all sorts of stories of his fighting days. He never really explained *why* he had to fight… but he fought in an old arena, to the death.

I suppose he must've been part of some criminal organization in the past. Strangely enough, even though he never openly told me, Nevaeh had basically said he was a eunuch, because when she said he had no balls… it most definitely wasn't an insult to his manliness.

I thought making eunuchs was something barbaric that old rulers did to their slaves?? Maybe it happened in an accident.

With all his stories about fighting, I believed that he most *definitely* could've suffered an accident or two.

He taught me a trick that could be used to even blind the foe with the sunlight reflecting off the blade. It was so dope!

We just used these wooden daggers in practice, but I showed him my butterfly knife I bought from a friend.

"Hm… These are very fancy… More flash and fire than substance…" Felix said, as he admired the blade.

"Ah, whatever, man. This is what they use in the movies! Ain't it sweet??" I said.

"As long as it feels like an extension of your body. I'd just get a good, strong, sharp knife, rather than one you can do tricks with."

He handed it back to me, and I swung it around in a circle, even throwing it up to the air spinning and catching it. I said, "I guess… I know you don't have to worry, with your old lady, Nevaeh… but I gotta get the chicks!"

He laughed, and said, "I never understood fighting for women. Nevaeh and I started our relationship because I showed a softer, gentler side, and did not try to fight. You should try to find this side of you as well."

"Pfft. Chicks like cool, hard as stone cats, like me. I'm thinking about asking Maggie out."

"Go for it. You can always show her your flashy knife move... and then cut yourself as you drop it." he said, and looked at me with an old grin, which seemed older than time, and I cut my hand on my knife.

"Fuck. Alright, I'll get something with a little more substance..." I said, as I held in the little bit of blood from the slight cut on my hand.

"Try to find the same in a relationship. Flash and show really are just a coverup for the strength and beauty within." Felix said, and we went back inside his new old house to Nevaeh.

8

I went out drinking with Renley and the guys on the weekend. Sure... we were just high school kids... but Renley's dad hardly noticed when Renley stole a few beers. I mean, they fought and swore like nothing else... but he probably wouldn't mind if a case of his went missing this time.

We drank and wandered around the streets. I threw up in the grass of this secluded neighborhood. No one cared if we did anything here! It was nothing like my neighborhood, always with the cops patrolling...

Damn cops. They never looked at me the same after I said I was raped by Georgia. I'm sure they just laughed and made jokes about it...

I mean, the guys all laughed and joked, claiming me as one lucky bastard when I told them about her... but she was my secret shame.

I was raped by a woman, and I finally saw that for what it was.

I kept on going to Yule's meetings, because we had something to connect about. We understood each other, all of us, and even though some of the women, like Yule, were *very* pretty, we weren't caught up in that. They still adored me, and I let them, but we all had been through that pain of having someone take advantage of us.

I called Maggie up, drunk to the gills.

"Heeey..." hiccup, "Mags. How's the... y'know... your best friend and crap?" I drunkenly said.

"...Are you ok? You sound a bit funny. She's just staying at my house. She... is just going through a hard time." Maggie said.

"Iiiii'm... Having fun! Yeah... You tell Tricia to get her own place! She's always making a muss of my hair when she has her way with it... I wish she'd juuuuust leave me alone..."

"She loves you, y'know."

"Whaaaaaat? That's bullshit, and you can tell her I said so." I said. Maggie hung up.

I shrugged it off... damn women... not even women, just teenage girls... not... like Yule...

After we had drank more beers, I went to Yule's house.

She invited me inside, looking at me funny as I was grinning, and said, "You feeling alright? You look like you had a little too much to drink."

"Iiii'm always..." hiccup, "Feeling alright! I misssssed you... for so long..."

"It's only been what, a week?" she said, and sat me on the couch, after I hugged her in drunkenness.

"I... I saw him again. I saw Stan."

"You mean he's still around? I'll get some of my friends, namely Dave, in the police force to look out for him... I don't like that he was a part of what happened to you in that club." she said, sat beside me, and continued, "You... Do you feel better now? Now that it is done with and over?"

I tried to kiss her.

She pushed my head back, and said, "Paul. You are not yourself... and you should know, I would never betray myself, or Max, like that. I don't think it would be appropriate to kiss you like when you were a kid anymore..."

I just grew tearful. I truly did love Yule... even if she was older than me... I just wanted her... instead of a damn succubus in my head...

She said, "It's ok." as I started bawling my eyes out.

Max came home, noticed me crying, and said, "Hey, Paul. You don't look like you're feeling very well. Want to help me make burgers?"

I said, "S-Sure." and went to the kitchen with him.

He chatted about his day in the kitchen, and allowed me to cut up some buns and toast them for the burgers. They were Antonelli's, the owner of the Italian restaurant, own fresh baked buns, and not store bought crap.

"Iiiii... love your old lady, Yule..." I said.

"I do too. I'm glad you cherish her as well." Max said, smiling at me.

"Buuuut... I like... *really* love herrrr... She's... I just feel so stupid..." I said, becoming embarrassed.

Max laughed, and said, "Don't worry. I get it. We've all had those hormones mucking with our minds telling us we love this one, and that, especially when we're young."

"Yooou're not gooonna kick me out? Or beat me up? Or sometttt-thing?" I said.

"Goddamn, no. I'm just going to tell you..." Max said, and put an arm on my shoulder, "That me and her have been through Hell and back. We've got a strong relationship, and... she won't ever use you like Georgia did."

"Oh... Ok... I get what you mean... You two are married and crap anyway... but Georgia was too... but I understand. Thank you, Max." I said.

He took his hand off my shoulder, and said, "Don't worry about it. I think it's great you're giving Felix company with Nevaeh in their new house. He's been a little lonely without his best bud, Maximus."

"I always thought it was weird how you and Maximus have such similar names. He, like, your twin or something?" I said, as Max fried up the burgers.

"Nah. But he's become a friend, a good friend, and is dating my sister. I hope to call him a brother one day." Max said, and flipped a burger.

"Felix is the best trainer I've ever had, I mean only ever had. It feels like I could take on anyone now."

"Well… your weapon can also be your disadvantage. Want me to show you a move I learned in a self defense class I'm taking?"

"Sure. As long as I don't hurt you or anything…" I said, grinning.

He laughed, and said, "I'm pretty sure I got this one down… but don't hold back! Here, take out your knife."

I did, and he told me to stab him.

"Wh-What?" I said.

"Just try it. I promise not to bleed like you did all over the table when Felix cut off your tail." Max said.

"I don't know about this…"

"I promise not to hurt you… Wouldn't want you to go crying all the way back to Hell, where you belong…"

I furiously stabbed at him.

He caught my arm with his left hand, pushed the blade past his neck beside his head, and held my arm in an armbar with his right hand on my joint. "I could snap your arm at the joint like this, if I wanted to. Your weapon was your weakness, and your weakness was my weapon." I stood there surprised as he held the armbar, but he let me go and said, "You're not a demon, Paul, so don't have to take insults like you are one. Just shrug it off."

I put the knife down on the table, and said, "S-Sorry. I just got so frustrated… Can you teach me that??"

"Sure." Max said, smiling, and taught me how to push the knife away, either down and away, or do a move like him and put the knife wielder in an armbar.

I said sorry to Yule for acting like a mule, and she accepted my apology.

We had delicious burgers, with tomatoes, onions, lettuce, ketchup and mustard, on homemade bread.

I left happy, knowing that Yule was in good hands, and that even if she couldn't protect herself, then Max could protect her.

9

I felt sort of like I was invisible in high school, even though the people, the teachers, the friends and enemies, were ten times better than the ones in grade school.

I decided to do something about my nonexistent noticeability, and got a big mohawk, poofy, with abyssal black hair like I always had.

Everyone noticed me and it, and I smiled as I flirted with the chicks.

They giggled as I allowed them to pet my hair.

Some older asshole named Dylan called out to me in the hall, saying, "Hey it's the spawn of the Devil himself. You suck off the Devil in an alley? What's the Devil's dick taste like, Paul?"

"Just ask your mama. I can never get a taste because she's always busy at it herself." I said.

"Bitch!" he yelled out, and walked away.

Renley laughed beside me, and said, "You shouldn't encourage pricks like that... Just do what I do and turn the other cheek."

"And then steal their cigarettes?" I said.

"Haha... No. I was a bastard talking to you the way I used to... But you gotta admit, we had pretty great fun as mortal enemies."

"Whatever happened to your little gang of minions?"

"They all went to the private high school. They... actually kinda abandoned me. I guess I deserved it..."

"Well, Renley, just know you've always got your best mortal enemy at your side."

"That makes me feel so much better… I gotta talk to Tricia. She's been having a rough time lately…"

"Why?"

"Oh… nothing. Just send her your prayers, ok?" he said, and went to talk to Tricia. They kissed each other, practically making out in the hallway, and then walked away hand in hand.

She still turned back to glare at me.

What? Was she trying to make me jealous? Not like I gave a shit about her. I shrugged, and went to class.

It was such a boring ass class… the teacher, Mr. Moleman as we called him, was droning on and on in a monotonous voice… so I said I wasn't feeling well, and went to the nurse.

Then skipped class, skipped going to the nurse's, and just dicked around with some other skippers like me.

They were all drug users and basically scum, but they were pretty funny.

For lunch, I didn't order a thing, and got my pass to walk down the trail beside the school and smoke cigarettes.

They allowed me to, since they knew some kids would smoke whether they liked it or not, so at least allowed them to do so in a free period. They just said I was "walking the trail." I just listened to the birds chirp and smoked my cigarette… It was nice getting a break from school.

Someone else approached from the other side of the path. Tricia, smoking a cigarette.

"Hey, Paul. You look like a punk with that haircut." she said, as we met on the trail.

"Hey, Tricia. You smoke too?" I said.

"Not only the cool kids smoke cigarettes, ya know."

"I guess not. Just the lost sheep like me."

"I guess that makes us a couple of lost sheep then… Well, I'm gonna go before I start falling asleep from counting all of them…" she said, flicked her cigarette butt in the woods, and walked down the path.

I thought of what Renley had said, that she was having a hard time. I had lashed out at her when I was going through my own hard time… so I said, "Hey Tricia!"

She turned back, and said, "Hm?"

"I just want to say sorry. I've been hearing you have it rough and I-" I started.

"What? Even *you* think you can pity me?? Even *you?* Just do another magic trick and disappear…"

"You know you messed with me first! You told everyone all those horrible stories about me!"

"I… I don't know! I didn't want them to know that I liked you!"

"Well go and walk amongst your sheep then. Follow your crowd into your own lonely little pasture… because that is the lamest thing I have ever heard."

Her face turned red, and she said, "I- You- I guess it is… Yeah… I thought it would be different in high school… but it's just the same…"

"What do you mean? It's great here! The only strict old ladies here don't even push religion down your throat! And half of the teachers are in their 20s even!" I said.

"Maybe it changed for you. But it just got worse for me. I know what happened to you… I heard about it from one of my dad and grandpa's customers… I'm sorry. I thought you were just being an asshole when you told me… But it really broke my heart." she said.

"…I… Hey! Don't feel bad about me! I had the time of my life! Fuck, I got action when I was ten!"

"I know you're lying."

"...Yeah, well, don't let everyone know... My friends think I'm a super stud because of it..."

"Just walk amongst the sheep, huh? Wanna walk back with me?"

"Sure, Tricia. Let's go back before lunch ends." I said, and we walked back in silence, together.

She mussed up my hair before she left to go to her classes, and I tried to fix it up just right again with my comb... Damn her... Why did she always do that...

I finished my school day, and walked back home with... Maggie.

She was a real chatterbox, and seemed to be caught in her own world of words coming out of her mouth. She would charge on through any-thing I had to say, but she was *hot.* One of the volleyball girls, and after Renley dragged me to one of their games... I could see why men like watching volleyball so much.

A bounce here! A bounce there! The ball went bouncing up and down! But not nearly as much as the players' butts and boobs.

Maggie was a hardcore athletist, doing at least one sport in every season. She offered for me to go running with her. I nervously accepted, and then she prattled on and on about something or other. I could look at those gorgeous lips wag forever...

I got up *early.* Way before school. Mags said that was the best time to go running, when the air was clean and the streets quiet.

I panted along behind her, her taking her time and slowing her pace for me. It was hard, no, impossible to focus on her beautiful behind when my lungs felt like they were about to collapse...

She was merciful to me however, and we walked for some of the ways.

But that was for not even a quarter of a block, and then she told me to get *my* beautiful behind moving!

I was dripping in sweat when we finally got back to my house. My mohawk was a soggy mess, and I stank like sweaty hell. I offered to drive her back to her house, but she declined, saying she'd like to get just a few more miles in.

I collapsed in bed and slept off my exhaustion… and when I got up, I was already late for school!

I thought about going in reeking like sweat, but Mrs. J, my homeroom teacher, would probably be merciful if I missed just homeroom…

I took my quick shower, checked my demon tail, and it was still a barely noticeable stump. I went to school.

It was a boring day, but at least it was a Friday.

I took Mags out after. While we were sitting to dinner and while I was admiring her hair… she said, "Are you even paying attention to me?"

"I really like what you did with your hair!" I said.

"…Forget it. Go talk to the birds." she said, and left as I protested.

I was stuck with the whole bill, and sighed that she bought the most expensive thing to order…

But the waitress, an older blonde woman who was very attractive, whose name tag said, "Darcy," said, "Go on, Saul. Get out of here, before the boss notices." and winked at me.

I quickly left. I didn't even have enough cash to pay for the full meal. We agreed we would pay for each of our parts separately.

I was walking through the door, and I realized that woman called me Saul.

I looked back, and she wasn't there. She seemed to have vanished, and the owner was looking at our unfinished meal and I vanished out the doors as well.

So what? She just was-

One of the demons of Hell.

And she helped me dine and dash.

So what? I guess I just had friends in low places… Shouldn't matter. They all owed me for putting me through that torture, anyway.

I was walking in the shadows home alone, and a voice whispered in my ear, *"We're all looking out for you, Saul."*

I turned, shocked at such a voice in my ear, and Stan was walking beside me, with a long hood over his head.

"Wh-What do you want?" I said, as I tried to walk faster.

He kept pace, and whispered, *"We just want you to go to your rightful place. We need you... for you are his blood. You are his kin."*

He didn't look at all handsome with the shadows on his face. It felt like instead of normal human features, monstrous features were looking back at me instead. I stopped under a streetlight, and he stood just in the shadows. I said, "What do you mean? Can't you just let me live my life in peace?"

He laughed, this horrible, evil, menacing laugh, and hissed, *"We just want what we deserve. A true afterlife. IS THAT TOO MUCH TO ASK?? You can give us peace from our suffering on Earth... You can wield the knife to stab your father in the back..."*

"I-I only have one father, and his name is Kasey." I said.

"And... if you don't do what I ask... you will have no fathers. Pick your father, choose your god." Stan whispered.

"Would you have me worship you, instead? To have me forsake all I hold dear to spend an eternity in the flames?"

"Only if that's what you deserve... and you look like you're going down that route pretty quick... So I ask you, as a lost soul, to help me." Stan said, and it looked like he was telling the truth.

"I-I don't think I can trust the King of Lies..." I said.

"Then you're learning well. You can only trust in yourself... But we'll watch your back anyway. Take my word! HAHAHA... And take this. Something with 'substance.'" Stan whispered.

He offered me a knife, a meticulously crafted steel blade with golden inlaid designs, and astounded by its beauty, I accepted Stan's gift.

"A true blade for a true knifeman. One that has shown up time and time again throughout history, and has only ever been improved upon... that only ever was forged in Hell. The metal it started with is the metal that Cain slew Abel in wrath, and this will be the blade you use to slay your father." Stan whispered.

"I-I won't kill my father..." I said, sighing as I knew I must return the blade...

But Stan whispered, *"Then it will be the blade you take your own life with. Take my blessings with care, Saul, Spawn of Sax..."* and he disappeared into the shadows, leaving me with the cursed blade.

I threw the knife into a drawer when I got home. I didn't want to think of what Stan said, and that knife.

I went to bed, and fell asleep...

And I was eating biscottis with the King of Hell in a park, sitting on a bench amidst trees and grass.

"Isn't Purgatory nice? I like to visit here when I can. Look, look there! That idiot has to amend kicking all those cats and now has to rescue them from trees!" Sax said.

"I thought you were the King of Hell? Why are we in Purgatory? Damn... these biscottis sure are good..." I said, crunching on a biscotti.

"I think it's a great place to amend my own sins. Of course, I always have to get back to work and torture the odd soul for a lifetime or two... but, penance feels good, y'know? Just makes me feel warm and fuzzy."

"The Devil wants me to kill you."

"We are in a park in Purgatory, not my domain, so you could never have an easier chance... but this is just a dream, anyway. Who knows if it's even real?"

"Yeah... I don't really want to... Even if you raped my mother."

"...I wish I never did. I only did… Well, I'm a demon. I kinda thought that was what I was supposed to do… I *did* enjoy it… but it haunts me. Your cute little face haunts me, still." Sax said, and finished a biscotti.

"I guess you are a despicable piece of demonic trash. I don't think I can ever forgive you, but hey, at least I don't feel like killing you. Not right now anyway. This Purgatory is nice."

"We, even you, have a chance at redemption. You may be my spawn, but you will always be able to go through Purgatory with me in charge of Hell. No more relentless trapping and torturing and suffering for pointless satisfaction… I actually enjoy less screams in Hell. Feels quiet."

"Alright. That guy looks like he's having a hard time reaching that cat. I'll go help him out." I said, and got up off the bench and went to help the man.

"Peace be with you, spawn!" Sax said.

I boosted the man up so he could help the cat out of the tree, and he thanked me for the help.

10

I stretched awake. What a weirdly pleasant dream. I felt safe with the sunlight coming through my windows… and I looked at the knife.

It really was a beautiful piece of craftsmanship. I ran a hand down the golden inlays, which strangely enough… were the sign of a detailed, golden cross. I ran a hand down the blade, and I didn't even feel the cut, but as I took my hand away my finger was oozing out blood. I frowned, and put the finger in my mouth and sucked off the blood.

It seemed to keep bleeding, so I bandaged the cut with some duct tape. I put the knife back in the drawer and got ready for school.

When I got into homeroom, I took off the duct tape, hoping it would be healed, but then blood ruptured out of my finger. A girl beside me screamed. I felt woozy, looking at all the blood dripping onto the table, and I fainted.

I woke up with a crowd of people around me, checking my vitals and nonsense, and I went to the nurse's with my finger bandaged properly. The nurse asked me if I was alright now, and asked me, "What the heck did you do to yourself? They said one second you're fine, the next you're bleeding out on the table!"

"Beats me. Just a little cut. I didn't realize I cut myself that deep… I thought it would've been healed by school time."

"You did just faint. Do you feel ok to continue going to classes? Or you can take a period to rest if you like."

I looked at the comfy bed, but I really was getting behind in some classes, so I said, "No, I think I'm fine. I'll go to class."

"Be sure to eat something at lunch and drink lots of fluids!" she said. I thanked her and left the nurse's.

I passed Tricia in the hall doing work as a courier for the school for her community service, and she smiled and waved at me. I smiled and waved back.

Then I noticed the bandage on her wrist.

I was going to ask her what happened, but she had already rushed off to deliver her papers and mail for the teachers.

I had lunch and ate a double helping of pizza. The pizza was the only thing that was really any good at the cafeteria, but I was starving for some reason and chowed down relentlessly.

I later asked Renley what happened to Tricia, and he looked away. He turned back and said, "Let's have a few beers and talk after school. Wanna come over?" I said sure.

We were drinking on his back porch. His family was all out doing things, and he said, "We did it, me and her."

"Congratulations! You're finally a man." I said, grabbing him around the shoulder and shaking him.

"Then she cut herself after I left." he said.

"...Oh. You were really that bad, huh?" I said, sipping from my beer.

"I didn't think so! I thought that's what she wanted! I thought it would make her happy!!"

"...You didn't pressure her into it, did you?"

"No. I don't think so... She was always kissing and hugging me, so I proposed we take it further... I don't know..." he said, chugging down his beer.

"Maybe take it easy for a while? Just let her heal off her cut?"

"She just… is telling me all this horrible stuff she thinks… about wanting to die. She never says so when we're around other people, but when we're alone… it's like she just put up a show for those people, and really she's only a shred of that happiness she displays…" Renley said, "I really can't deal with it. I'd break up with her, but I wouldn't want her to do something crazy if I did."

"Maybe you just have to let her down easy? Buy her a full course meal, tell her nicely that you and her should just be separate, and just be supportive? *I* couldn't deal with depressed people… Honestly, I don't know what I'd say to them. I'd say, 'Hey! I was raped by a succubus! You think you have it bad? I'm the Spawn of Sax!'" I said, and drank at my beer.

"…Spawn of Sax? That your band name or something? Sounds pretty cool… but… that was the only time you've ever admitted to me that you were raped." Renley said.

"…Yeah… You guys all looked up to me for it, thought it was cool… It is one of my worst memories. She made me feel… like my body was rippling with pleasure, and then… she took it all away. It felt like I fell from Heaven." I said.

"…It was that good? Tricia and I could never get the positions right!"

"So good, it was awful."

"Well. I don't think I'll ever get there with Tricia… I'll let her down easy and break up with her, because if she keeps doing crazy shit, I'm gonna end up losing my mind too."

He got a text, buzzing coming from his pocket. He looked at it, and said, "…What? Tricia…"

I said, "What? Is she ok?"

"Yeah… but she just broke up with me… with one, stupid, random text!!"

"Well, you got what you wanted, right?"

"I- Grr... I just... Whatever. Let's drink some more and work on those stupid essays for Moleman." he said, finished his beer, and threw the can into the backyard.

Dana was being a brat with her bratty friends after Renley and I stumbled back to my house, after getting pretty well started on those essays, and talking about the band we wanted to make. Dana and her friends teased us relentlessly, and Renley was practically falling over at Dana's flirtatious remarks, but I said, "Quit it, you succubus. Where's Dad's old guitar?"

"You're not gonna scratch it up and break it! Go be a good boy and be quiet in your room. Renley can hang out with us." she said, and her friends giggled.

Renley said, "Really?? That sounds kind of fun-"

But I said, "They just want to do your hair and put makeup on you. Happened to me when they asked me to 'hang out,' and I quickly turned into their doll. They even wanted me to wear a dress!"

Dana said, "You'd look sooo cute as a woman, Paul! I think that's your calling. What's your size, Renley?"

Renley said, "...Uh. Well I don't know anything about dress sizes-"

"I'm thinking you'd look great in pink." Dana said.

I told a blushing Renley to come to the garage with me, before they could drag him away, and there I found it, Dad's old guitar, laying on the old couch in the garage.

I played the thing, jamming out some notes, and Renley listened. I just jammed and jammed! I didn't know anything about guitars, and I just made it up as I went, but I kept going, and it sounded *kinda* like a song, I guess.

"Sounds ferocious, Paul. But give it here... I can tell you don't know shit about guitars." Renley said. I handed it to him, and he strummed out notes like that was God's purpose for him.

"I never knew you could play guitar!" I said.

"Learned it when I was a kid. I can teach you some chords and stuff, if you like." he said, and handed the guitar back to me.

"Sure. I guess we're gonna need more people, unless we want to be some ridiculous lone duo." I said, and stared at the guitar.

"Yeah. Can you sing? I know that basically anyone *can* sing… but not everyone *wants* to sing… like me."

"Sure. I *did* always sing in church… I guess that's as much training as I really need, I suppose."

"As long as we don't become some crappy Christian band. Like we discussed, we're going for Black Sabbath, Judas Priest, Metallica type shit."

"Well… Mags does take band, is fucking percussion since she wanted the easiest job and still get the credits… but hey, maybe she could be a drummer? If she was fucking speaking to me I'd ask her." I said.

"Really? You two broke up? Hm… I can ask her, if you just say sorry for whatever BS you pulled." Renley said.

"Sure. Although I don't really know what I did… Although I guess I should've been listening to her and I would've known…" I said.

He laughed, and said, "Probably just that. You gotta *listen*, Paul! Will help with our band, anyway."

I laughed and said, "Alright. Let's just start with a drummer, and we can just jam for a while and make things up until we find what we want to shoot for."

We shook hands, and started the band.

11

I apologized to Mags with Renley, and she said to me, "...Alright. I forgive you. I'm still not getting back together with you though."

Renley said, "He's already moved on. Want to join our band? We need a drummer."

She said, "...I don't think I'd have time... I don't even have a drum set, anyway..."

Renley said, "My brother had one that he left when he went to college. I'm sure you could use that."

"...I don't know... I don't really ever use the big drums in practice... But *you'd* let me use the big drums??" Maggie said.

We laughed, and said she could use whatever drums she wanted to.

"Alright." she said, "But we better not be practicing in some smelly old garage or something."

I coughed, and said, "It's really not *that* smelly..."

"...Fine. See ya, you dorks." she said, and smiled, leaving down the hall.

We continued the day, and I was really getting excited for this band. I had music in my head, in my body, just dancing along with me. I practiced a song I was making up in my head, and then I heard this beautiful sound coming from the band room during lunch.

I peeked inside, and Tricia was practicing her saxophone.

She shook off a piece of hair in her eyes, and said, "Oh, heya, Paul. You come to laugh at the band geek?"

"No! I thought that was astounding! I know you're in my lunch, but you never seem to show your face around the others. Wouldn't have guessed you spent that time either smoking or playing saxophone." I said, and walked into the band room.

"Yeah… I just don't really like being around other people… I prefer being by my lonesome most of the time…"

"What happened to those gaggle of friends you used to have?"

"They're all bitches, anyway. And they expected me to be head bitch, so that they could all say, 'At least we're not as bad as *her…*' so I told them to go suck a dick. I have no friends…"

"What about Maggie? You two are always palling around."

"She's cool, I guess… but she just thinks I'm some idiot… She's never said so, but I know she just feels bad for me like everyone…" she said, and looked down to her wrist with her healing cut.

"I don't think so. Want to hang out with me, Renley, and Maggie this weekend? We're starting up a band." I said.

"…I really don't want to talk to Renley…"

"I, er, know you two got intimate-"

"What? Is he telling *everybody* now?? He slapped my ass like a pervert!"

"…That's really not so bad as some things-"

"*God…* I just wanted to die right then and there… and then I tried to! Everything just- and he didn't even believe me when I told him I was going to kill myself!"

"Not everyone knows what to do when put in those situations-"

"And now he's telling everyone, and everyone thinks I'm a slut now!!" she said. She was breathing very quickly.

I walked up to her, as she was clutching her saxophone and hyperventilating, and I said, "Look at me, Tricia." She looked me in the eyes, and I just stared calmly back into them.

"...You really do have pretty eyes." she said.

"You don't have to come to practice with us. But maybe just you and I can hang out? Talk? I don't really know what you're going through, but I've been there too. I thought my soul belonged in Hell for the longest time." I said.

"O-Ok. Are you asking me out??"

"Um. I think we can just be friends."

She sighed, calmed down, and said, "Ok. I still have your number from grade school."

"I… deleted yours… Call me sometime?"

"Yeah. Thanks for helping me calm down."

"Anytime."

"So you did like my little performance? I practice the saxophone day and night, really. I think we're going to put on an astounding show in the jazz band." she said, and put her saxophone back in its case.

"Jazz. The Devil's music, not like what we're going to play, heavy metal… I really liked your song!" I said.

"Ok. Well, it's a solo that I am playing. Do you want to see the concert?"

"Sure. Sounds neat. I'll bring-"

"I'll save *one* seat for you with the band kids. It's at 6:00. Don't be late!" she said, and smiled.

I smiled back to her.

I listened to Tricia's breathtaking solo, sitting in the seats alone where the jazz band kids would sit after their performance, and then wait for the concert band kids to play their music.

It felt like she was singing through her saxophone, like she laid bare her soul for all to admire.

I applauded loudly with the rest of the crowd when it was finished.

She sat next to me, and gosh, she sure did have pretty eyes too. When we were kids, it was her growing breasts which attracted me most. But she sure had pretty eyes.

We sat and listened to the concert band, Tricia whispering in my ear critiquing it here and there, saying that kid could really go a long way if he practiced more, and that that kid really just needed to let loose her spit valve on her trumpet.

I hung out with the band kids afterwards with Tricia, and God... they were *weird.* But they all got each other's inside jokes and didn't seem to mind as I looked at them funny. One got me into their shenanigans, and soon I was acting just as weird as them, laughing all the more because of it. I could see why Tricia liked this cast of oddballs and goofs. They didn't try to hide their flaws, or expose other's weaknesses. They just accentuated their own oddities, and let the world give a damn.

Tricia grabbed my hand with the saxophone case in her other, as we walked back home.

I said, "I-I won't try to-"

"Don't make a big deal out of it. Just something I always wanted to do." she said, and we held hands. We broke off at a corner, and I bid her goodnight, walking back home alone.

But there was always someone following me, whispering in my ear when I walked alone these days...

Stan, the Devil, and he whispered, *"What if she gets raped while you let her walk alone? You should really be more supportive..."*

I tried to punch him, but there was only darkness where my fist swung at.

He was over my other shoulder, and said, *"I can't wait for the happy ending with her. You can baptize her in my name..."*

I swung again, but there was no one there. I walked home in silence, cursing Stan to Hell. *"That's exactly what I want, Saul..."* he whispered.

I just ran the rest of the way home, running from the Devil.

12

Maggie was just getting used to the drums, but beat out rhythms like that was something she always wanted to do. She finally got what she really wanted to do in band.

Renley rhythmed out some guitar, like he always felt his place was here in this band.

I strummed my dad's guitar, sang out growling, roaring, but still with Maggie and Renley, singing my song.

I sang, *"I'm Saul, the King of Hell, and I know you ain't doin' so well...*

But I want to say you're really making me feel swell, the way you're doing that way...

Jamming to the rhythm, like God could give a damn,

Jamming to the rhythm, like Satan cursing at the lamb...

Like fixing a dishwasher, swearing at the rhythm..."

Maggie continued her beat, smashing the drums and banging the cymbals.

Renley continued his growing chords, getting more complex as we continued.

I sang, *"Play your sax, I'm the son of it,*

Play your song, as we continue the chords...

As the drummer beats the rhythm, like the goddamn Lord's...

We're playing for you, and you make me feel good...

Nothing like a succubus from Hell ever could."

We just jammed and jammed! We really never wanted to stop, but eventually got tired. Maggie missed a few beats, and Renley was starting to strum out random notes. I told them it was time for a break. They sighed out, and I got us some sodas from our cooler we set up.

Maggie said, "That was so much fun!! Jesus Christ, I never knew you two who went to a Catholic school could be so cool!"

Renley and I laughed, and I said, "We have to make up for our shitty education someway."

Renley said, "I thought you were really great on the drums! Everyone needs a good drummer."

"I think you were so cool on the guitar! I mean, Saul tried to keep up... but he's really much better at using his voice." Maggie said.

"Wait, Saul?" I said.

"That's what you said in the song, right? I thought that was pretty cool." Maggie said, and slurped at her soda.

"Yeah, I guess... Just something someone used to call me..." I said.

"Well fuckin' hell, Saul! It's like you have a different personality when you're singing! Like you're really a king of Hell. It's pretty dope!" Renley said.

I smiled, as we drank soda and just relaxed for a moment.

Then we got our second wind, and Renley burned the guitar, Maggie burst apart the drums, and I sang my soul out.

We were all tired when we finished. I never knew singing could make you so exhausted! Renley and I each hugged Maggie goodbye, as she said she had to catch volleyball practice. She was going to her car, as Renley looked at her fondly, and I said, "Go get her."

"You're alright with it?? Ok. See ya, dude!" he said, and went to Maggie basically confessing his true feelings She invited him to come with her and he accepted. They got in her car and drove off.

I just smoked my cigarette, happy for my friend.

I got a call from a number I didn't know, and I answered.

Tricia said, "H-Hi,"

"Hey Tricia! How's it going?" I said.

"…You remember my voice?"

"Well, duh, I'm not gonna forget you."

"…Thanks, I guess. I wanted to ask how the practice went."

"It was great! Maggie really blasted those drums, and Renley strummed out his heart." I said, smiling at our practice.

"…That's nice. She's been saying all sorts of stuff about your band… I mean, good stuff. She really has a place for you in her heart…" Tricia said.

"What, Maggie? She drove off with Renley just a second ago."

"…Oh. I thought you two would work out your differences."

"Nah." I said, "I just said sorry for not listening to anything she said… I don't know what is going on through her head sometimes."

She laughed, and said, "I feel that way sometimes, too. Although… I really thought you two would end up in Heaven together… You really did look nice, you and her."

I laughed, and said, "No way! She always liked these really tight pants I wore! It really got annoying, when she asked me to wear them every day… and I couldn't even feel my balls breathe."

"Balls breathe?" she said.

"Er… You know! Like when you sleep with your socks on. You gotta let your feet breathe."

She laughed, and said, "That's pretty ridiculous. But I think I get what you mean." We just kept on talking about silly and mundane stuff, and I felt happy as she said, "Ok. Well, I'll call you again, Paul. Take care."

"See ya, Tricia." I said, and we hung up.

I exclaimed in anger when I saw the new cut mark on her wrist the next day. She said, "I-It's nothing... D-Don't worry about it."

"You don't have to hurt yourself! You're great! I don't know why you can't see that!!" I said.

"I-I... I don't know... Just walk with me, ok? I don't feel so good." she said, and I held her hand.

She thanked me for the company, and I said, "If you ever feel like hurting yourself again, please call me or someone, ok?"

"O-Ok... I honestly- Just feel better when I do... Like... happy, in a weird way..."

"That's just because it releases endorphins in your brain, making it habit forming. You should try to quit the habit." I said, doing some research on cutting and worried about Tricia.

"Ok. It's hard to quit a habit... W-Would you mind... just being with me after school today? That's when I feel like cutting myself the most." she said. I said that nothing could stop me from being there, not even the Devil.

Even though the Devil mocked me the whole time I was going to her house, with his gang of demons. Telling me to join them, telling me to help them rob a liquor store...

I just knocked on Tricia's door, and she answered. She asked me who were those men on the other side of the street.

I said, "No one. Just forget about them... Please. They don't belong here."

She shrugged, and let me inside.

She showed me her knife... which was the same exact one that I had.

I exclaimed in shock, and she said, "Used to be my grandfather's, and my father's, but it was passed down to me... They just wanted me to protect myself... But now- I can't get rid of it..."

"I- I can give it a good home. I can make sure it never haunts you again." I said.

"I don't know… I could never do that to a family heirloom…"

"I- I'll just hold onto it. Until you feel safe again. I don't want you to hurt yourself with anything."

She looked at me hopefully, took the knife out of the case, and said, "It's worth a fortune at least… but… if you can make me feel safe… Just hold onto it for a while, ok?" and handed the knife to me.

I shoved it into my pocket, its hilt sticking out of there.

She hugged me, and said, "Thank you for giving me some peace." I hugged her back, the weight of the knife in my pocket.

We just talked, even had some awkward pauses for a while, but we charged on through them and I could really see that Tricia, despite whatever she did to me in the past, was a truly beautiful soul.

I cursed Stan, for causing her suffering, her father's suffering, her grandfather's suffering.

I hugged her goodbye.

How many knives were like this one in the world? How many knives were there to take the owner's, and even their family's, lives?

I wanted to throw the knife in the trash, this worthless piece of garbage, but I kept it.

I showed the twin knives to Yule.

"So this is a knife of Hell, eh… Looks just like any ordinary knife… even with the crass golden cross on the blade…" she said.

"I… just want to get rid of them… but Tricia places some value in hers, keeps it, despite the suffering it causes her… I can't believe it's the same as mine."

"Your suffering is not really unique. The person behind that suffering is, but everyone suffers in the same way. We all hurt, we all feel pain… and we all have knives of the Devil, in our own way. Do you want to leave them with me?" Yule said.

I shook my head, and said, "It is my suffering, my cross to bear. And I'll bear it gladly! If I ever see Stan again I'll kill him with his own blades."

"Just forget about him. Let him suffer his own way, as I'm sure he is. Throw the knives in a box, lock them up if you have to, and just keep them for another day. Hopefully you never have to open that box again." she said.

I nodded, and when I went home I did lock them in a strong case I bought, and locked them tight. To change it up just a bit… I put the lock number as 665.

Our band days continued, and it was the thing that made me feel alive the most. Even with Stan tormenting me whenever he could…

But I was safe in the garage, with the music, with Tricia. She came over one time and played her sax for us.

We just let her jam with us, jammed with her as she let loose on her saxophone. She never talked to Renley very much, but she didn't have to with Mags and him taking up most of the conversation. During our breaks, Tricia and I just sat together in the old lawn chairs in the garage, as they prattled on about something on the couch.

Later in her room, Tricia showed me the bass she got. She jammed on it, and said, "I've just started learning, but it's really not *that* much different than a saxophone, I guess."

"Holy shit!" I said, admiring her and her bass, posed in a rock and roll position, "We could actually have a chance at making a real band! This is so fucking dope. You're really, really fucking cool!"

She smiled.

We held hands on her bed, as that was what she liked doing, and I happily noticed she didn't have any more cut marks on her wrist. Those two long scars were enough.

We coughed, clearing our throats, "Er hem, er hem, er hem, er hem…" then couldn't stop each other from kissing each other over and over.

We did things like when I was raped by a succubus… but it didn't feel like rape. It felt like love.

She kissed me goodbye, blushing and smiling, and I smiled happily. It felt like I had truly made love with a woman then.

She still didn't have any cut marks on her wrist the next day.

Then, Tricia, the girl I hated for some of my childhood, was my girlfriend.

We flaunted it! We reveled in it! Let them all see our suffering, and our satisfaction!

Tricia got an award for her jazz performance, and I continued on through my studies. Tricia told me to study extra hard, and well, she kind of helped me do so. We studied together.

The study breaks with her were like bliss.

13
——

I had left the guitar in the garage again, and when I came back... I found Dana singing and playing guitar.

"I amm... a backdoor man..." Dana sang, and strummed on her guitar.

I just sat and listened. I kinda thought that since no one was using it, the guitar was kind of mine. Dad didn't play it anymore, and I always wondered how it got to the garage...

Dana turned, smiled, and said, "Heya, Paul. I never get a turn on this thing since you're always breaking the strings on it. How many have you broken, anyway?"

"Er... not that many... That was sweet." I said, talking about her music.

"You can have it back now, as long as you promise not to bust it apart in some stupid rock and roll move..." she said, and tried handing the guitar to me.

"No, I'm not really that good at it anyway. We have Renley to play guitar, and Tricia is getting badass on bass. Keep it." I said.

"Alright... But you're missing out on getting rock and roll powers from the Devil or some crap..."

"Nah. I'll just shout at the Devil, right? Can you play me any more blues?"

"Sure. I love the blues. I learned about it in a black history class, and I could never get it out of my head after I started listening to it."

"Blues. Now that's *really* the Devil's music, right?"

"Nah. Some cultures think all forms of music played publicly is basically Satan, so I'd say anything that people dislike can be called 'Devil's music.'" she said, twanging the guitar.

"It sure is better than that poppy crap they play in the halls at school. *That* is basically Stan- I mean Satan."

"Oh I can't stand that stuff! It's something little girls are supposed to like or something. Whenever I play on our school radio station I try to sneak in the good stuff, but that's few and far between." she said, continuing playing.

"How is that job, anyway?" I asked.

"Eh. It's kinda boring really. I can't wait to get out of this hellhole town and go somewhere nice... Somewhere like the big city, where Mom and Dad grew up. Or maybe south, where it's warm all the time. I don't know, anywhere but here."

"It's really not that bad... There's just hardly anything to do."

"Pft. Everyone knew about you and that Georgia woman... but still, no one did anything about it. They all learned from their crappy small town gossips and snitches, and *still...* they couldn't catch her. You mentioned that she was the wife of a boxer?"

"Yeah... but don't worry about it. I'm not some idiot kid anymore... and it's not like it's gonna happen again." I said, and started a cigarette in the garage.

"I swear to *God* if I ever see her... I'll make sure she burns in Hell for messing with my little brother." she said, and twanged out some more notes.

We just sat while she played like that, and I believed that Dana would take Georgia back to Hell. I knew no one could mess with my badass blues sister.

Later, Tricia and I were having dinner at a restaurant, and I saw... Georgia, and her husband, a big man, *way* bigger than me.

The big man lit up in jealousy when Georgia whispered in my ear, telling me *to meet her in the back alley and lose the innocent doe...* talking about Tricia.

I lit up in fury. Tricia lit up in fury, and Georgia laughed demonically and went outside to have a cigarette.

I was walking back to my house with Tricia, and Tricia said, "...That was her, wasn't it."

"I'm going to kill her."

"What? No, just forget about it. Just let it be, please." Tricia said, getting worried for me.

"I-I... You don't understand! You'll never understand! I'm a demon of Hell!" I said, turning to Tricia.

She held my hand, and said, "No. You're just my Paul."

"I need to end this. I need to have some sort of satisfaction. I need to get rid of her... and if I don't come back, know that I love you."

"No, Paul. If you love me you'll come back! Don't- Don't go there! Please don't!" Tricia said, and held my hand harder.

"Alright. We're home. We're safe now. You're safe now..." I said, and we walked into my house.

Tricia hung out with Dana, as they chatted about some girly crap, and when they were distracted I went to my room.

I clicked the number 665, and opened the case, revealing the knives. I took them out, and snuck down the stairs.

Tricia called out to me, but I ignored her. I must meet my own nightmare, and I must end it.

I found Georgia making out with her husband in the alley.

"It's your challenger, dearie." Georgia said, and her husband cracked his knuckles and walked up to me.

"You're not going to get away with raping my wife." he said.

"...The fuck?? She raped me! I was ten years old!!" I said.

"Stop your bullshit, you idiot teen. I'm going to kill you." he said, and swung at me.

I stepped back, but he still caught me in the swing, smacking my jaw. I held onto consciousness and drew my knives, a fire in my eyes only to match those of the fires of Hell.

He stepped back as I slashed at him. I had weapons... but he didn't really need any weapons. He was much bigger than me, had muscles of granite, and could probably take my head off with a swing of those fists if he wanted to.

We warily circled each other.

Georgia cackled and taunted us, saying that the *big man better kill the loser...*

The boxer swung at me.

But like Max had done to me, I caught his fist with my arms, wrapping the knives around them...

And I cut off this boxer's right arm at the joint.

He screamed, bleeding everywhere, his arm fallen to the ground, and I walked to Georgia.

"I'm going to kill you, you succubus." I said. I realized my voice was cold and hollow, as I was finally getting my dream fulfilled.

She giggled and ran off down the alley. I chased her.

I looked around the darkness for her, and she tackled me from the shadows, concealing her entire form in darkness for a second. Her true form was revealed to me, a creature of Hell.

I could not move my arms, as she held them down. She was stronger than even the boxer.

"That's right, Saul... I AM MUCH STRONGER THAN YOU WILL EVER BE... I am Georgia, your ever living nightmare... I will make my mark on you

PERMANENT... FOREVER. As people admire your features... they will see only my mark. As women love and adore you... they will only see me." she said.

She clawed at my left eye, leaving large cuts as I screamed.

I swung my freed arm with the blade at her, and stabbed her in the gut.

She gurgled up blood, and laughed, saying, *"And your fate is sealed... Have a good death, Saul."* and she died, but was slowly burning to ash, a creature of Hell.

I had killed my rapist.

I had cut off her husband's arm.

And now I was damned to Hell.

Stan clapped from the darkness, and said, *"You better come with me. I wouldn't want Dave in the police force to catch you... He's quite a good soul, and hates to see people die... Come with me."*

I followed the Devil in the darkness, sheathing my blades as my face bled from the claw marks.

Part 3: Acedia

Sloth

14

The Devil and I ate trash, we stole booze from stores, we sheltered with other lost souls like us.

I missed my own graduation, on the run from the law. I was permanently Saul, no longer a human, only a demon trapped on Earth.

The claws coming from my toes and fingers proved this, if anything. I'd always try to hide them under big boots and gloves that we stole... but still, they would always cut through, would always show themselves on accident, and the random passerby would stare at them for a bit, before shaking their head and walking quickly away.

My demon tail had regrown, longer and thick, like a whip with a spike at the end of it, and I hid it in my pants for most of the time, unless I needed to lash it out at the random, crazed addict and make them regret ever meeting a demon.

My horns were growing stumps, but I hid them under my growing hair.

People tried to beat me, kill me, tried to chase me out of each town, but I always held my ground, with a broken booze bottle, with my tail, claws and horns... and if I needed to, my knives.

We wandered the U.S., and I asked Stan if we were ever going to reclaim Hell.

"In time... just enjoy living suffering on Earth for a bit... It's what God wanted for all of us... Revel in sloth..." Stan would say, as we warmed our hands from a trash fire he lit with his flame.

I was thankful I was basically invisible… and no one noticed me most of the time. I was truly not even supposed to be here. Stan showed me how to make people betray their beliefs, their sight, anything, and I would truly be invisible then. None could see me, as I walked amongst them, none smelled me… even if I smelled myself, and I smelled awful, like brimstone, and the Devil and I walked the Earth.

I daydreamed about the life I had given up… pitying myself, hating myself… wishing I could go back to Tricia, my mom and dad and Dana, Yule…

But I was damned.

I saw Yule looking for me. I knew she was, she was showing my picture to everyone she met… and I cloaked myself in shadows, walking past her.

She caught my arm. She could see through any trick of mine or the Devil's, she could see me.

Stan told me to run, and I did.

Yule caught up with me. She didn't particularly look like it, but she was stronger and faster than anyone I've ever met.

Stan summoned his legions of Hell to assault Yule.

Minions trapped on Earth, endless rats, demonic forms, sprung from the shadows and clung to Yule, scratching and biting at her sides.

She screamed out, "I'll destroy you all!!"

Brilliant, white, bursting flame lit from her, blazing the trainyard we were in in brilliance, lighting every dark corner, and scattering the demons to the shadows.

Her eyes blazed with that light. She turned to me, and said, "Come with me, Paul."

I did not want to meet my maker. I did not wish to feel the wrath of her God.

I threw gravel in her eyes which blinded her momentarily, and I ran as quickly as I could.

I got to a quarry, and tripped off the side, rolling downwards to the pit.

As I continued to show my true form, my *demonic form...* shredded demon wings, like a large bat's, erupted from my back, and I flew.

I soared! It was a remarkable feeling.

But I saw the angel, Yule herself, jump off the cliff to meet me.

Her own angelic wings sprung from her gracefully, not even tearing apart through her clothes like mine had done.

She chased me through the sky.

I flew upwards, past the clouds. I was a demon, and this was the closest I would get to Paradise.

Yule flew before me, cutting me off, and I halted, hovering in the sky.

"Come back to Earth, Paul." she said.

"I am Saul, the Spawn of Sax, and I belong in Hell. Will you take me there?" I said, and in a quick move, as she was distracted by my words, I took out my blades and slashed at her.

She raised her hand, and a sword of Heaven caught the blades.

I flew backwards, as she burst forth flame and light from herself, and I flew in the darkness.

She was like a supernova! She sundered the sky with God's light!

It was impossible to evade that light eventually, as every darkening bit of sky was enlightened.

The light hit me. I felt paralyzed, and I fell through the clouds, dropping my blades to Earth.

Down, down, down... way back to Earth, probably all the way to Hell...

But Yule had caught me before I hit the ground, and she carried me in her arms down to the ground.

I looked at her, a true angel of Heaven, as she carried me down the street.

She told me it would be alright.

I fell asleep in her arms, a strangely restful sleep, with no dreams. It felt like I had died, but I woke up, and Yule set me down in front of my house, careful not to hurt my wings and tail.

I instantly hid my true form. I did not want my *family...* if I could truly call them my family, to see me so wretched.

Yule rang the doorbell, and I cowered before my family that came to me... and they immediately hugged me.

Dana said, "My *God...* You look just awful!! You look-" and she started crying, and crying, and my parents took me gently inside.

Yule blocked off my escape, and waved us goodbye.

My parents just kept on hugging me! I told them, *"I'm not your real son... You don't have to care for me. You're not my dad, Dad, and you never wanted to have me, Mom... Just let me pass into the shadows..."*

My dad, Kasey, said, "No. We know you only fought in self defense. That woman... she was the one... who *ruped* my son..."

"I'm Saul... I can never take back what I have done... I can never undo it... I will always be the Spawn of Sax..." I said.

My dad said, "Paul. It truly will be alright. Georgia- was never found... The only thing is that boxer... saying that you cut off his arm and killed his wife... He's suing you for taking his livelihood, but he has no evidence. The case will be thrown out."

"I fought for vengeance... I fought-" I started.

My mom said, "You only wanted peace, and that woman still didn't let you have any... Oh... those marks on your face... It looks like you've been fighting wild animals or something… Please, let's just clean you off. Into the shower, chop chop!"

I said, "…Like a baptism or something?"

"Much more pleasant. You smell… really bad, Paul. Just wash yourself and you can sleep in your bed in your room. We didn't touch a thing. Dana even put off moving, so we could all look for you. You don't know *how* worried we were!" my mom said.

I smiled and broke down crying.

My mom led me to the bathroom, and gave me privacy so I could wash off the stink and tears.

So the case was going to be thrown out. They had nothing on me. So… all that time… I was running from nothing. I was running with the Devil, from just my own fears.

I had eaten roadkill. I had drank water out of the gutters. I had to shelter with drug addicts and scum. I ran from dogs and police sirens.

All that time I lost, and I was running with the Devil!!

And all I had to show for it was a missed graduation and a claw mark over my eye.

I breathed in and out in anger in the shower, hating Stan, and it was almost as if I could hear him laughing at me.

But I suppose even though the Devil tried to take everything from me, he couldn't take the people who cared for me. He couldn't take the people I loved.

15

The warm shower felt nice on my wings, tail, and claws. I hadn't had a real shower in ages.

And a real bed was much better than the streets.

The first thing I did in the morning was make myself look presentable.

I filed down my claws, my horns... Not really much I could do about the wings, and the tail actually was kind of nice. Gave me just a little bit more balance, so I just poked it through my pants and hid the hole, tail, and the large bat wings, from people's sight with my demonic trickery.

I suppose I could just walk around looking like demonic trash if I wanted to, but I smiled to myself as I looked into the mirror. I at least needed to do this for myself. I combed back my long, black hair, and then shaved off the beard.

Dana was taking college courses from home, but delayed them to talk to me and watch me with my mom and dad. My dad even took a few vacation days, just for me, so he could spend time with his son.

I just smiled tearfully as they gushed their love, and I gushed back. They, although I thought the opposite, never thought of me as scum, a monster, as a demon. They just thought of me as Paul.

I told them all about the horrible Hell on Earth that I went through. It felt like I was reliving it when I told them, and they asked brief questions or exclaimed in shock.

"Thank God for Yule. She had called and said she found you collapsed, and carried you all the way back to us herself... God bless that woman. I don't know why... but I swore I saw angel's wings on her. God must've put her on Earth himself." my mom said. I smiled and nodded. I told her I wanted to thank Yule for saving me.

Dana said, "I'm coming too. I really don't want you doing *anything fucking stupid* again, ok?" and we went out the door. Dana gave me her favorite red scarf, saying that'll keep me warmer from now on. I thanked her, and pulled it up over my mouth and chin.

We walked in the brisk cold, and I asked Dana whatever happened to Tricia.

"She... found someone else. She looked for you with us over and over again, but... I think it was just too much for her to bear." Dana said.

"Oh... And the rest of my old band?" I asked.

"Went to college, I'm afraid... Renley and Maggie send their love however. I called them up when you were sleeping. God, you slept like you never wanted to leave that bed..." Dana said.

"It'll be nicer dying in my bed, rather than on the streets..." I said.

"Don't *ever* talk like that. You're not gonna die young. I swear... I'll put you in a hospital if you even show *a hint* of wanting to kill yourself..."

"...Alright. Thank you."

We knocked on Yule's door, and Max answered saying, "Uh... Can this wait? Yule... is... just... fixing her hair!"

"We can wait." I said.

Max sighed, and said, "Oh- Never mind... Come inside. Just please don't scream, ok, Dana?" and he led us inside.

There, we found Yule trying to hide her angel wings under a big coat. She looked pretty ridiculous.

"...What's that on your back, Yule?" Dana asked.

"N-Nothing! Don't worry about it!" Yule said.

Dana rushed to her, thanking her for saving her brother, and surprised, Yule unfurled her angel wings and the coat went flying off her. Dana stepped back, mouth agape in shock.

"Y-You're really an angel." Dana said.

I sighed, and said, "And I'm a demon, Dana. I've been hiding it from you the whole time... but just *look at me now...*"

She looked at me and I snapped my fingers, revealing my true form. She stepped back, knocking over a side table, and stammered in shock.

"Y-Your horns... your t-tail... your *wings...* This doesn't make any sense... I-I... am crazy." Dana said.

Max said, "This never made any sense... But no, you're not. I married an angel, and your brother is the son of a demon."

"M-My dad's not- Oh. Yeah... Paul has a different father... Yeah..." Dana said, growing sad.

"I still think of you as my sister, Dana." I said.

"...And you'll always be my brother. But- you're really supposed to be in *Hell??* How- How can God let my brother burn for an eternity!!" Dana said.

Yule started to say something about free will and the like, but got caught up in her words, so Max said, "Let me take this one, Yule. Your brother doesn't belong in Hell. Yule doesn't belong in Heaven. While we live, we belong on Earth. Let's just think about where we should go after we've finished our time here. Let's just enjoy the moment, and not get caught up in the afterlife."

"...That makes me feel only slightly better. The tail on Paul does not." Dana said.

Yule said, "I think... when Purgatory was blocked, it caused all sorts of disruptions on Earth. We're all the aftermath of that, us demons and angels. I *could* try to get them all where they belong... and then go to Heaven myself..."

"I like what Max said. We're gonna die sometime... so let's just not worry about it, ok?" I said.

"...Alright. I wasn't really sure where to start, anyway... and I hate slaying demons. I know, that's strange... but an angel of war like me needs to be merciful. That's the only type of war God can ever wage, a merciful, just one." Yule said.

Dana sat on the couch, and said, "O-Ok. Got any beer, Yule? I need a drink."

"Yeah. Let's drink... I had to quit my job, quit volunteering... and everything sucks. People see me as an angel now! How can I live incognito with giant, bursting, fluffy feathered wings? I honestly didn't think I would ever get wings again, but I needed to go after Paul... and I had faith when I leapt off that ledge." Yule said, and got us all some beers.

She handed me one, and I said, "I could show you how to... trick the viewer. Make them only see what you want them to. It's worked for me plenty of times.

"You mean lie?" Yule said, sipping on her beer, "No, no, no... I won't do any Devil tricks to keep my place on Earth... Max and I will just move to Nova Scotia or somewhere, somewhere where no one will see, or care... Just be an angel on Earth..."

Dana said, "I'd move to the big city. No one gives a shit what you look like there, even if you've got giant wings sticking out of your back."

"Hmm... I would like to see Maximus and Fate again... What if we just had a short trip, and figure out what to do when we get back?" Yule said.

"I really like that idea. I've only been to a few big cities with the Devil... and they were easiest to get around in." I said.

"Yeah. Let's make an adventure out of it." Dana said.

I went back home with Dana and went to my room, just to relax in a comfortable place for a second... I heard a buzzing coming from the phone that I had left before I went to meet Georgia, recharged again after I plugged it in.

It was a number I didn't know, and I answered.

Tricia said, "H-Hello?"

"Tricia?" I said.

"Ohmygodohmygod… You're back!! You're fucking alive!! I-I… Can I come see you?" she said.

"Well, I look like a- Are you sure?" I said.

"Yes. I'll be by in a sec! Just- Just don't go anywhere!!" she said, and hung up.

I answered her relentless knocking, and she immediately hugged me to death, even kissing me on the cheek a bunch. She grabbed my hand and seemed to never want to let it go. I took her to my room so we could talk in private, and I filled her in on what happened to me. She said, "I thought you were dead. I thought you died in that alley. But you came back. You do love me."

"D-Don't you have someone else these days??" I said.

She took out her phone, sent a brief text, and said, "Not anymore. I love you, Paul. You *fucking idiot asshole stupid piece of shit boyfriend!! How dare you go off and leave me!! For idiotic, stupid, vengeance!! Next time I go anywhere with you, I'm going to put you on a leash so you don't run off like a goddamned hound!!*"

"…I love you too?" I said.

"Good. Now remember that." Tricia said.

16

I did everything I could to help out around the house. Anything, before Yule, Dana, Tricia, Max and I went to visit Max's sister, Fate, and Maximus. Nevaeh and Felix were touring the country, but I called them up and Nevaeh said, "...God. You demons and angels really live confusing lives... but stay safe, ok? Talk to people first instead of being blinded by rage."

I talked to Felix about the knives of the Devil, and he said, "My own worst nightmare, what actually brought me my doom, was fighting and killing. It's great to freshen up self defense lessons... but it should only be that. Fight to defend, not to kill or mutilate. The only way I ever would've had my family and friends I do now is because I put down the blade."

I thanked them, and did the dishes again.

Tricia was hanging out with me while I did housework, and said, "You don't know all the *pricks* I went out with... I had given up on you... but this last guy, instead of sympathizing with me for you... instead goes and tells everyone about how my 'last boyfriend was a real douche, a psychopathic spawn of the Devil...'"

"So you never did give up on me, then. You were holding me in your heart, as I was holding you in my heart." I said.

"...Yeah, I guess... It felt shitty leaving you. I skipped out on going to college just to look for you, you know. But everyone told me to move on... and that I was wasting my time on you..." she said.

"I'm sorry, Tricia." I said, and I sat at the table with her and held her hand, "I wish I never wasted all that time... and I wish you didn't have to waste yours for me. What are you up to now?"

"I'm just working with my dad and grandpa. The restaurant is nearly 70 years alive and strong! I can't believe my grandpa is still making pizzas and Italian food like that... but my dad is really getting everything moving along swell, and my grandpa is going to pass the restaurant down to him. I'd love to be a part of the family tradition... even though that's *a lot* of responsibility... but I'm just not sure I want to spend the rest of my life being a waitress..." Tricia said.

"Ever thought of being a chef?" I asked.

"Yeah... but I've cooked for you before, and you know, I can't cook for shit." she said.

"Hey! I really liked those ham sandwiches!" I said.

"Yeah. Just ham on plain bread. 'Bout the best thing I can make, really. I'm sure one of my brothers and sisters will take up the role, instead." she said.

"Alright. Max and Yule should be here soon. I'll go get Dana. Love you, Tricia Antonelli." I said, and kissed her.

I knocked on Dana's door, and she said, "One sec! If I just... There! I've gotten weeks of school work done ahead of time! I'm all set to go!" and she opened the door and smiled, with a backpack over her shoulder.

The three of us chatted with my parents for a bit, and they said as long as we're with Yule and Max, we'll be fine.

I smiled and hugged them goodbye as I saw Max's car drive up. "Have fun, dears!" my mom called out as we left.

Yule had these badass black shades on, and looked out the window to us and smiled, a cigarette between her fingers. Her wings were scrunched into the seat. We got into the car behind Max and Yule, and I scrunched my own wings into the car. Tricia knew Max and Yule from when they were out searching for me, and said to Yule, "Um. Neat outfit? Are we going to a convention?"

"Hmm… Are there angel conventions? Oh, Max! We should go if we see one!" Yule said.

Max laughed, and said sure. We drove off down the road.

We just listened to music. While we were on a busy street a car cut us off and it startled Yule, and she burst out her wings making Max swerve around for a second.

Then the siren blared behind us, and a cop pulled us over.

He was going to give Max a ticket for reckless driving, but took one look at Yule smiling politely at him with her fluffy, white wings, and said, "Uh. I'll give you a warning this time. You should really take those things off if it distracts the driver."

He then walked back to his car, rubbing his eyes.

The others laughed, as we continued to our destination. I stared out the window forlornly.

Would be nice to be an angel… showing hope and friendliness, being true evidence of a just and good god, invoking faith in others…

But if I showed my true form, all I would invoke is fear.

Tricia noticed me with my pitiful, sad expression, and just held my hand. I squeezed hers tight.

We drove, we talked, we drove, we talked. It was actually a nice break from things.

We got off the expressway and drove into the big city.

We parked for lunch, Max had a little difficulty parallel parking, but got it in the end.

When we were walking into the restaurant, a demon walked out.

Yule and I were immediately on our guard, fist ups, ready for a fight.

But the demon man said, "Woah! Neat outfit, lady! Those are some high quality feathers!"

"Outfit?" Yule said.

"Oh, you're one of the roleplayer types. Isn't it such a cool game??" he said.

The demon paint on his face was a bit smudged.

"I'm on my way to the convention now! You just look... badass! Your skin and hair is like, completely white too!" the man said.

"I'm actually an albino." Yule said.

He laughed, and said, "I'm the demonic lord Tubano! Cool. I'll see you guys there!" and he walked off humming some song.

We sat down and had cheeseburgers and talked. I said, "That game fest... would be kind of fun... I actually wanted to get that one game where you go to the netherworld and become lord of the abyss... heh... before it came out... but then everything happened..."

Yule said, "We'll check it out."

Tricia said, "As long as there's not *too* many costumed nuts around. Like- Are there even going to be any women there? I feel like us gals will be kind of alone in the sea of testosterone..."

Dana laughed, and said, "You wouldn't expect it, but guys and gals love to do a good bit of cosplaying. It's like an extra Halloween, and some really go all out for it. I was dating a cosplayer before... and *she* was *hot* in that alien outfit..."

"Wha-What??" I said, "Y-You never mentioned you were gay! Kind of a big thing to drop on someone!"

"I guess I swing more to *the attraction of the heart...* Everyone already knew besides you, Paul." Dana said, slurping on her soda through the straw.

"...Oh. Uh. Congratulations?" I said.

Dana shrugged and smiled.

We checked in at our hotel, and set our backpacks down. Tricia, Dana and I in one room, Max and Yule in another, and we got ready for the convention.

I breathed in and out a bunch… walked into the bathroom, snapped off the illusion… and showed Tricia my true form.

She was admiring the demonic parts of my body, feeling the leathery wings, feeling the sharpness of the horns, and I tried not to show any reaction as she tugged on my tail. "Wow. I didn't know you were a full on nerd too! You wanted to go to this convention from the beginning!" she said.

"Uh Y-Yeah. That was the whole reason we went on this trip!" I said, smiling nervously.

"Only if we had time." Dana said, helping me lie.

Tricia and I held hands, and she didn't even mind the claws! I breathed out a sigh of relief, and Tricia said, "It must take courage dressing up for a gathering like this. I'm glad you could be the real you."

We went to the convention, with hordes of demons, angels, aliens, and other casts of characters and creatures.

No one minded that I was myself here! I just wanted to flap around in the sky in joy, but I just walked around with our group as we checked out all the new games and comics.

People were super interested in Yule, even though the only thing she "dressed up" with was the wings. Her skin condition and star tattoos were permanently stuck to her. I think the interest had partly to do with her just being super nice and friendly on her own.

People smiled at me, and thought I looked cool! I smoked outside with Tricia and a bunch of other "demons" and they talked about their own achievements in the game, which bugs there were that you could exploit, and all sorts of nerd stuff.

The "succubus" was even one of the nicest people there, giving Tricia and I a beta pass for a game she was making. Tricia looked at the piece of paper with the passcode funny, but I smiled and put it in my wallet.

Max bought a whole bunch of comics, finding super cool ones that he's never even heard of before. Yule tried a VR game, and actually really kicked ass in it, as she wielded her virtual sword and shield. Dana was flirting with a couple of Italian plumber girls, and I never knew that she was hiding something in her life like I had been. Even Tricia thought the place was neat, seeing my normal side and other things she's never seen before.

We walked back to the car, really enjoying the convention, and as Yule and Max were getting in, I looked up to the sky happily, up to the big skyscrapers… and I saw someone plummeting to the earth.

I broke free from Tricia's hand and launched into the sky.

The man was screaming, but I caught him in my arms. Then he looked at my demonic form and screamed some more.

I set him gently down onto the ground and he ran off.

Yule, Max, and Dana ran up to me. Yule said she'd catch him and calm him down.

Dana hugged me, saying thank you for saving a life. Tricia slowly walked up to me, blinking a bunch.

Tricia started a cigarette, didn't say a single word… and just stared at me in awe.

Yule had convinced the man to go to a hospital, actually walked him there too, and we went back to the hotel. Tricia was still staring at me in awe in our room.

I sighed, knowing I must hide my true form again…

But Tricia grabbed my hand as I was going to don my disguise, my human self.

She said, "I don't understand. But can you keep the costume on? If it'll help you sleep better."

I smiled, and took off my clothes and slept beside her, moving my tail, wings sticking out of my back.

She shivered at the tail touch, but as I wiggled it back and forth playfully, she stroked it, and slept with it in her hand.

<h1 style="text-align:center">17</h1>

I woke up to Tricia frowning at me with my tail still in her hand. The sunlight was shining through the windows, and Dana was still snoring in her bed beside us.

"Shouldn't it have disappeared with the rising sun or some BS? Like a vampire?" she said, still frowning.

"I'm not a vampire... What kind of vampire gets woozy at the sight of his own blood and faints?" I said.

"You mean... *even back then?* But- I still don't understand..." she said.

"Well, I'm a demon-" I said.

"No. Just let it be a secret. I don't think I *want* to understand this mystery. As long as you're not like this all the time..." she said.

"I am... I just hide it sometimes." I said.

"Oh... That must kinda suck. But the flying thing and saving a dude was fucking cool. You should really keep track of all those lives you've saved. You've at least got two souls in your pocket now, that one guy... and me." she said.

"I lost the knives... both of them- got lost." I said.

She sighed, and said, "Probably for the best. Please hide- this... from other people. But you can show it to me."

I smiled, put on my pants with the hole for the tail, my shirt with the huge holes ripped in it for the wings, and we went down to breakfast.

I allowed Tricia to see the real me.

It was our little secret, and I tricked everyone else but her and our group to see me as a normal 18 year old boy. Tricia and I were kicking each other slightly under the table. I poked my tail at her, and she said, "No fair."

People didn't really mind Yule's wings in the city. They thought she was just another street performer or actor or something. We actually stopped to listen to a street performer, a one man band who said he was Odin. Max put a ten in one of his instrument cases, and Yule and him had a conversation about their respective afterlives, how they differ and the like.

We got to Fate and Maximus's building, and took the elevator to their apartment. They lived up high in the clouds, and they opened their door, smiling to us and greeting us. They looked like they were doing rather well in this big apartment for the two of them.

Fate took us to the living room, and Maximus got us some beers. Fate said, "None for the children, dear."

"Oh! Right. Forgot about that law here..." Maximus said, and got Tricia, Dana and I some sodas.

Dana asked, "Do you come from Europe or somewhere?"

Maximus said, "...I... lived in Europe for a while, yes. I'm actually a Roman- I mean, an Italian."

"How's the football career going, Maximus? Did you ever get that big win, that win to set apart all the others yet?" Max asked.

Maximus said, "We've been having a good season, but I haven't found that rush to beat even the old days. Although, the team is great. When I used to be in the colosseum of old, I was alone."

Tricia asked, "What do you mean? Just not enough comradery in sports before?"

Maximus said, "...Well... Uh... Yes."

Fate said, "We really love this city. It's far different than a small town, and we had a hard time making friends at the start… but there's so many people! New ones of all types wherever you like! It makes even that cult look small!"

I said, "Oh yeah, you wrote something about cults? What's that all about?"

"It is an unpleasant memory for me, so I will not rehash it again, but here, if you like, I detailed my entire life experience with cults in this book, and have helped put together an organization to help others out of manipulative entities like that cult that I used to associate with." Fate said, and handed me a whole book she wrote called, "The Cruelty of Calmaog and Cults."

I read the back as the others talked. It said, "Calmaog was love. Calmaog was life. And Calmaog took each of those things away from me when I joined his church. There was no life to be had, imprisoned in our dull clothes, all the same, there was no love to be had, as our god forced himself on all of us and sold our bodies to the highest bidders, one who we gave our souls to for free.

"This is the story of how I eventually freed myself of their chains, mental and physical bindings, and how the cult was eventually destroyed by my sister-in-law."

Her sister-in-law… Yule?

They were talking about charities and the like, donating time for others which Yule missed doing, and Yule said, "I wish I could just do more." She didn't seem to know she had already done so much. All those people she saved, me included, and they were all saving other people because of it.

We all went out in the evening to a performance, to some college musicians playing who were called the "Thieves of Belfast."

We stood in the stands, and in the dark on the stage the drummer started up a beat. The lights went on... and the band roared out rock and roll.

I looked harder at the drummer, with her new pink and black dyed hair... and I saw a familiar face beat out the rhythm, smashing the cymbals and pounding the drums.

Maggie, our old band drummer.

Tricia and I approached her when the performance ended, and the band was cleaning up their instruments and the people were leaving.

She was making a little beat on the cymbals, then noticed us, dropped her jaw at us, and rushed to Tricia and gave her a huge hug, as they both squealed in glee.

She turned to me, and said, "Hey, you. I'm glad you came back to life." and hugged me too.

"You're a drummer for a real band now! I'm so happy for you!" Tricia said.

"I thought we *were* a real band?" I said.

"We were just high school punks. Maggie is getting *paid* for her music!" Tricia said.

Maggie coughed, and said, "...Mainly just dinner. But it's all you can eat!"

Tricia said, "Huh? Oh. How's the studies? Do you have time to hang out with us?"

The others were chatting about the music. Maggie looked back at them, and said, "Uh... We have to stop by the restaurant before it closes... but maybe you two can stop by our house?"

"Sure. I'd love to see how you live now!" Tricia said.

"...Yeah, I bet you would... Alright. Well, come with me... and see how I live..." Maggie said nervously.

I told the others we were going to hang out with our old friend, and they said they could pick us up later if we liked.

We followed Maggie to the restaurant with her band. They were all older college kids, studying music in their last years. I wondered how a college freshman got in with such an experienced crew?

We stopped by the restaurant and ate this incredibly adequate Asian cuisine. But, there was never an end to it, and the band and Maggie ate like it was their last… or first, meal.

"These two aren't going to be narcs, are they?" the guitarist asked.

"Oh hell no. They're from my old band." Maggie said.

"Good. I gotta pick it up. I'll see you guys in a sec." he said, and kissed Maggie on the lips and left.

Oh. So she was the guitarist's girlfriend. That's why she was in the band. I thought she played great anyway, even if she didn't have as much experience as these people.

We got to her house where the band all lived, and they had a party.

The bass player slapped Maggie's ass, saying she played really well.

Maybe it was a harmless slap?

Maggie laughed, and said that they kicked ass.

We drank a bit of booze… and Maggie and the singer were making out.

Oh…

Tricia and I just stared around nervously, as the guitarist came back with "it."

Maggie and the band got down to a snort of white powder, and offered some to us. "Don't be narcs, ok?" Maggie said.

Tricia said we should really be getting back to the hotel… So we left, hugging Maggie goodbye.

She smiled as we waved her goodbye, looking back at her with the guitarist holding her around the waist.

"Oof…" Tricia said, as we walked back to the hotel.

"She always- did- look really good… I guess she finally found a way to spend it?" I said.

"Kinda makes me glad I didn't go to college, and have to end up hanging out with scum like that." Tricia said.

I sighed… and said, "At least she's got a roof over her head and is eating something…"

"Eating the band's dicks. Fucking idiot. As soon as they graduate she'll never see them again." Tricia said.

"At least we saw her again. There's something in that. Right?" I said.

"I guess. Let's just hold hands and not think of ours and others mistakes. You big demon boy." she said.

I smiled, holding her hand, and said, "Want me to fly you back?"

"Y-You can? Th-That sounds fucking cool." Tricia said, and nodded up and down.

I picked her up in my arms, and flew her with my demon wings. She was clinging to me for dear life, but she relaxed after a bit, knowing that I wouldn't drop her. We looked down at the streets with all the people like ants, and flew to our balcony at the hotel. I set Tricia down and she was laughing in delight. We knocked on the balcony door and Dana let us in.

"You silly goofs." Dana said, "You could get in trouble if you fly around all willy nilly!"

I said, "No one noticed us, it's like we weren't even there. No one can see me but who I choose…"

"And I choose to see you forever, Paul, my guardian demon." Tricia said, stroking my cheek. She kissed me, and we sat on the bed to watch TV.

18

I had kind of been in Maggie's shoes before. I had to associate with all sorts of lowlives just to survive with the Devil, but I never did so just for *fun*. I still called her again with Tricia, and got her to agree to visit her parents and us back in our small town when she gets the chance.

We drove back home. It was a nice trip, and I couldn't have picked anyone better to spend a few days of rest with than Tricia, Dana, Max and Yule.

Later, Tricia and I went to Maggie's house, and we saw Maggie swearing at her father on the porch. "Forget it. I'll suck any dick I want! Even if they're *horses*!" Maggie yelled, and charged to her car.

"What?? Young lady! Come back here right now!" her dad said. She flipped him off, and drove away.

We talked to her dad for a second, and he said, "I… just want her to get a good education… and not have her be taken advantage of like she's a tramp!! I'm- sorry that I yelled at her…"

"You can tell her that. She probably just needs to let off some steam. We'll go find her." I said.

We found Maggie at a bar, drinking with a fake ID.

We sat beside her as she hiccupped into her drink, and she said, "Whaaa… Oh. It's the demonic duo… Youuuuuu look kinda like a demon, Paul…" and blinked at me.

I worked extra hard to hide my demonic form, but she still tugged at my tail. She shrugged it off and slurped at her drink.

Tricia said, "So… how's the agriculture major? You wanted to do something with animals, right?"

"Iiiii fuck like an animal in beeeeed… But they still think of me like I'm some side piece! Like I'mmm their fleshlight in the shooooower…" she said, slurring at us.

"Um. You don't want that, do you." Tricia said.

"Iiiii had so much fun when I firsssst started! Butttt… the gangbangssss… just aren't special anymorrrrreeeeee… I'mmm just having fun! I spent alllll that time working on my boddddy… and I only got two people to really appreciate it, oneee bastard… you, Paul, who didn't hear a thing I saiiid… and Renley, my stupid ex… I feel bad forrr that idiot girl he knocked uppp." Maggie said.

"Renley got someone pregnant?" I asked.

She patted my cheek, and said, "Yoou always hear only the last thing I sayyyy…" and slurped at her drink.

I said, "No. I heard it all. I just think it sucks. Sucks like-"

"Gettting molested? It's nothing like you. You idiot twat. Youuu fucking fucker! You wasted all that time, left us for some idiot whatchamacallit… for your molester! You left us toooo get molested again! Was it that good, Paul?" Maggie said.

Tricia said, "You leave him alone."

"And you. Always thinking youuuu have it sooo bad… You didn't have any responsibilities. No oneee gave a shit what you diiiid…" Maggie said, sipping at her drink.

"I have lots of responsibilities. You just can't see them… because you're drunk and trying to fuck your own problems away." Tricia said.

"I love you guysss… I really dooo… I just am so angry! I wish I could just cut off theeeeir arms like Paul does!" she said.

"That really won't make you feel any better." I said.

She started crying, saying that they were getting a new member of their band… and that she'd probably have to fuck him too…

"What if you just got away for a bit? Take college classes at home?" I said.

"They're getting a drummer! I'm nothing but a fucking hole for dicks to them!! I… just want to quit…" Maggie said.

Tricia said, "College isn't for everyone. I mean… if that's what you want, you can. You can always go back another day."

Maggie passed out on the bar, and we carried her out.

We got to her parents' house. She had regained consciousness, but was still woozy, and lost consciousness again as she tripped to the couch. She kind of halfway was on it, so I helped her get settled, and Tricia tucked her in with a blanket. Maggie's mom thanked us.

Later, Maggie called each of us and apologized. She said to me, "I really think that one thing you said about horses was pretty magnificent."

"What? I never said anything about horses. You said something about horses to your dad." I said.

"…Oh. Well, I'm dropping out. I guess if you and Tricia are still around… we can play like in the old days? Just have fun?" she said.

"That sounds great, Maggie. I think you've really gotten good on the drums!" I said.

"Yeah, well, I had to practice beating- drums. Just drums." she said.

"…Oh. Ok. Well, come on over sometime, and we can make an event out of it." I said.

"And… I think… you're really… looking bigger these days. You're as attractive as the Devil now… with that long black hair…" she said, trying to flirt.

I sighed, and said, "No, I'm just a demon of Hell."

"…Well… that's pretty hot. Hot as Hell, eh? You don't know how attractive that is when you demonize yourself like tha-" she said.

"I get it, Maggie. But I'm dating Tricia, your *real* best friend. We both care for you." I said.

"...Oh. Ok. Alright. Just don't remember anything I said, ok?" she said.

I laughed, and said ok, and we hung up.

Even though we played again, and Maggie was a lot better at drums now… it just wasn't the same. We had all changed, and I sang a sort of somber song,

Maggie stopped drumming, and said, "Seems… a bit depressing."

"Yeah…" I said, "I want to get back into it, and your bass is cool, Tricia, but we've got no guitarist."

Dana was listening at the door, and said, "Can I play with you guys?"

"Sure. We could be like the Doors and make sort of bluesy rock." I said.

Dana got her guitar, and she asked if Maggie knew "Break on Through."

She started up the cymbals, and Dana rocked on the guitar. Tricia improvised on bass, and I think it actually sounded cooler than the actual song. I sang what I could remember from the song, adding in rhymes and things differently if I felt like it.

It began snowing outside, as we continued to cover the Doors.

Dana said it was fun, but said she had to work on some extra work for college. She left us and smiled to Maggie, and Maggie smiled back.

"Your sister is pretty hot. Makes sense that she's a lesbo." Maggie said.

"...Uh. How does that make sense?" I said.

"Girls know what girls like. Make sense?" she said, beating out a beat on the drums.

"...So… you like my sister?" I said.

"I wouldn't mind taking her out. I've experimented, was one of the first things I did, and she's like, a *real* chick. Not some butch. I kinda like that." Maggie said.

"...You sure got more balls lately. You just say what you think. I can't believe I never noticed that." I said.

"Eh, and you got more sappy. I remember the old Paul secretly told me he wanted to be a *gladiator...* Fighting and killing. You got your wish when you cut off that guy's arm." Maggie said.

"...You know there's no proof of that..." I said.

"But it happened, right? Fucker had it coming picking on a teenager with his rapist wife if you ask me." Maggie said.

"...Thanks, Mags." I said.

She smiled, and stared deeply into my eyes, then winked.

Tricia got a little red at that, and Mags said she was going to talk to Dana.

"...There's not something between you two, is there?" Tricia asked.

"No, but she is giving me eyes and flirting with me... Now she's talking about taking out my sister!" I said.

Tricia put her bass back in its case, and said, "I suppose it's harmless if it's Maggie... It's harmless, right?"

I held her hand as we sat on the couch, and said, "Of course. You don't know how long I've been wishing just to hold your hand again, not Maggie's, not someone else's.

She held my hand, and said, "You didn't fuck ladies of the night when you were 'running with the Devil?'"

"I kind of did think about it. But... you don't know how terrifying it is letting people see the real me, a demon. I honestly was just terrified I would accidentally slash someone to pieces with my claws if I got intimate with someone..." I said.

"Is that why you haven't advanced when all signals say 'go?'" she said, and smiled.

"Er- Yes. How about we make a date? I'll make sure my claws are filed down to nothing." I said.

"It's ok, as long as you're careful with them. You're like a giant tiger with them. Rawr." she said, and swiped her hand like a cat's at me.

I smiled, and we made our date.

I was wrapped with Tricia, she was wrapped with me, and my tail was wrapped around her leg.

I accidentally cut her with the tail spike. I said sorry a bunch, but she told me to keep going.

We bandaged her up after, and she said, *"God... It's like you were in prison or something, just waiting for a good woman."*

"Er... Is that a bad thing?" I asked.

"Not at all. Just means I gotta ration out the loving so you don't burn up from lust..." she said, grinning.

I grinned, kissed her again, and she pet my tail.

I walked back home from her house late in the evening... and I was truly alone. No Stan, no demons, no nothing.

I was finally happy for a while, even being a demon on Earth. But I saw glinting in a gutter, and picked up... the knives.

Both of them were still there, and I knew then, my suffering must continue.

Stan said, *"It's time to go to your rightful place."*

I looked back at him next to a man with a bull's head, and the bull man sucker punched me.

I lost consciousness.

Part 4: Invidia

Envy

19

I heard someone say, "Just do it quick, ok?" and walk up the stairs.

I woke up bound to a chair in a basement. The bull man was in front of me, and mooed at me.

The woman who helped me dine and dash, Darcy, was watching as the bull man hooked me up to the generator.

I panicked, and tried talking even with the gag in my mouth.

Darcy said, *"Shh. Be quiet, Saul. We just need to invoke a near death experience for you. So you can go to the afterlife and kill your father."*

Stan walked out of the shadows, lighting a cigarette with his flame, and said, *"Your Father in Heaven, Saul."*

I just stared at him. Then it clicked. He wanted me to kill God. How was that even possible?? I just mumbled under the gag.

The bull man mooed at me, and Darcy cackled.

Stan continued, *"You see... We, as lost demonic souls, have no way to get into Heaven... You thought we wanted to go back to Hell?? Let Sax keep his eternal prison. I envy his ignorance... You will be accepted into Heaven... being such a mortal lost sheep. I'm sure the shepherd will welcome you into his pastures gladly. But this sheep is a wolf. As soon as you kill one man, one gatekeeper, we can get through to Heaven. You must kill St. Peter, and God, and Jesus, and all of their bologna saints. You will ascend to Heaven, and kill your Father."*

106

I shook my head.

He sighed, and said, *"I thought you were one of us... I thought you cared... Well, I promise to kill your human father, your family, Yule and everyone... in your name if you don't do this."* and he tricked the viewer, he used his demonic trickery, and showed... my face. He laughed, and said, *"That Tricia... she just thought it was so nice after I came back for seconds... She cried when I slapped her ass and held her down..."*

I felt my heart sink to my stomach.

"It's only an afterlife. I promise we'll be out of your hair forever, if you help us do this. If you don't, you won't even have a life to live." Stan whispered.

I felt the tears in my eyes... and I nodded.

"Blast him with electricity, Molech." Stan said. The cow man mooed, and I was electrocuted.

I felt myself pass. I saw my body, but I felt lost. I didn't know where to go, as it seemed like dense mists were surrounding me. Would I go up? Or down? Or just stay here?

A demon walked to me in the mists, and said, "Heya, spawn. I'm so glad you're dead! We can have so much fun together." I told Sax, the King of Hell, my father, that I needed to go to Heaven. Sax said, "Are you sure? We can really have fun torturing this one guy... He beat his wife and drank himself to death. Now she beats him! It's fun seeing people get what they deserve."

"I... I need- to kill St. Peter..." I said, and looked down at my knives, somehow passing with me to this limbo.

"Because of something Satan said? Fuck no, they killed you and laughed at it. You can't go back." Sax said.

I felt my heart... not beat.

"Here, just follow me down to Hell, and I'll see if you can amend your short, pointless life when we get to Purgatory..." Sax said, and I followed him down the stairs to Hell.

I followed him over the screaming bridge of souls, and he took me to the lowest pit of Hell.

It actually wasn't so terrible. Looked like he redecorated a bit.

I stared at the green, lively Christmas tree, and asked him why he put it up so early.

"Oh, I just really like that holiday. 'Bout the time I came to Earth, anyway. And people hate seeing it up all year round... Makes me chuckle." Sax said, "Want to watch TV? I introduced it to Hell, and our stations... are terrible! It's wonderful."

He sat on his big King of Hell throne, and I sat on the sofa.

We watched people do horrible things to each other, humiliate each other in unpleasant ways, and then they got up and did even worse things to their tormentors. Sax laughed his ass off at this horrible program. I looked at him and he said, "Vengeance never ends... I wonder when these saps will learn that? It's funny seeing them cycle through the loop over and over again..."

I looked back at the TV.

"So... this is my hell? Watch TV forever with the demon that conceived me?" I asked.

"It could be worse. You lived a pretty lukewarm life. Started a band, had a girlfriend. You could've done so much more... So, now you don't get to do anything. Just until you've learned from your mistake." Sax said.

I stood up in anger, and yelled at him, "*My mistake?!* My mistake followed me through my life! And I could've never done anything about it! *My mistake was being conceived by you!!*"

"So you kept that original sin, you let it follow you around and dictate your choices. Ever heard of baptism, Paul?" he said.

"Baptism?! I was 'baptized' by the Devil! And it was the worst experience of my life!!" I yelled.

"Hmm... And you still let it dictate your actions. A lot of people would give anything to make love to a gorgeous woman like that, and then they'd shrug it off and just call it an experience." he said.

"You- Grrr... But I killed her! I finally got my justice, and then had to run from *myself...* the whole time!" I said.

"You're still doing the same thing. You're letting the past make your future. It sounds like you're stuck there." he said, sitting on his throne, "Georgia's not so bad, when she's burning forever. She cried forever when she got here again... Did killing her make you feel justified?"

"I... I... I don't know... It didn't make me feel any better, it didn't take away what she did... Just made me even worse off..." I said.

"Exactly. You can't just go running around killing people, even if they wronged you. Now you know why you're *really* here, you fucking spawn scum." he said, and smiled.

I sat back on the couch.

"Even though she's a demon from Hell?" I said.

"You are too. Would you like it if someone killed you because you cut them off on the highway? Vengeance never ends. It's funny seeing you cycle through the loop over and over again..." he said.

I looked back at the TV.

But then I noticed the Yule tree. It had wilted.

"How long have I been here?" I asked.

"A good three years so far. And we've had the same boring conversation every time. I think it's pretty great. I never knew my spawn was such a boring piece of shit. You make me proud." he said.

"I... I understand. May I... talk to Georgia? Tell her I'm sorry?" I said.

"Sure! We've never done that before!" Sax said.

The Christmas tree fell over, long dead.

We walked out of the pit and Sax relieved the demon torturer working on Georgia. Georgia's intestines crawled back into her body and her skin unflayed itself.

"H-Hi, Georgia." I said.

She looked surprised to see me.

"I'm sorry… that I killed you. You didn't l-look too good, with your skin off you like that…" I said.

"Why should you care? It's not like you had any reason to love me. I wanted you to despise me, for my own satisfaction." she said.

"And you fucked a kid for fun?" I said.

"Why else?" she said.

I sighed, and said, "I know you probably don't care that I'm here… But I didn't get any satisfaction from killing you. It was… just awful. I wish I could take it back."

She said, *"…Fine. I really did get you down here, eh? Shouldn't I get a promotion, Sax?"*

"You know that's not how this works…" Sax said.

"Well. Did you just come to do the same thing to me? I mean, you're all grown up now. You may actually enjoy yourself." Georgia said.

"N-No. That sounds awful. I-I hope your soul finds peace, eventually, even though we're in Hell." I said.

"Hmph. Maybe I am in Hell… Why does he get to have only a trial of the damned life?" Georgia asked Sax.

"I can't let him get nothing for being my shit spawn. Family perks." Sax said.

"What do you mean?" I asked.

Georgia said, *"You're not dead, dude. And I'm not just trying to torture you again…"*

"…I'm not?" I said.

"You've been in a coma for a good three years. I think it's time you go back now…" Sax said.

"Why didn't you tell me sooner??" I said.

"You just needed to know a little bit more about where you come from. I think you've learned your lesson, so… just take it as an experience. Back on the rack, Georgia! It's time for the tickle torture!" Sax said, grinned, and snapped his fingers.

20

I gasped awake in the hospital bed.

Tricia was holding my hand, but gasped as well.

She stumbled back out of her chair, and ran out the door. I blinked a bit, blinded at the lights, and said, "Tricia?"

She peeked around the door frame, and said, "Y-You're dead."

"Uh, no. I feel just awful and would really like some water, though." I said.

She filled up a cup in the sink, and gave it to me, cup shaking, and let me sip from it.

"I-I… Ever since you said those awful things… In that cold, hollow voice… I thought you died then. And then you did. I-I abandoned you. I did things with other people… I left you like this." she said.

"I don't expect you to sit with me forever while I'm in a coma…" I said.

"Ohgodohgod… You knew you were in a coma?? I said such awful things to you!! Ohmygodohmygod… Please forgive me." she said.

"I forgive you. Thank you… for visiting me?" I said.

"I-I just- think it sucked, and was feeling nostalgic… Even though our relationship ended on a down note…" she said.

"I'm- sorry that happened. Even though it was that asshole fucking hellwipe… He- didn't hurt you, did he?" I said.

Her face grew pale, and she said, "I didn't even let you- him, in. Who tried to murder you?"

"Him. Stan the Devil." I said.

"O-Ok. I-I… still don't understand. But I need to tell someone about this. I'll be back later, ok?" she said, slowly pecked me on the cheek, and ran out the door.

Soon, my family was all hugging and kissing me, crying tears of joy. Tricia wasn't there, but Maggie was, holding Dana's hand. My dad said, "My *son*... My son is alive again."

My mom said, "God has given us a miracle."

Yule said, "You poor baby… You good little angel… You didn't lose…" and hugged my head.

Max punched me on the arm, and said, "The eternal gladiator would never stay down."

Felix and Nevaeh cried tears of joy, and watched me smile in happiness at everyone.

The hospital checked to see if everything was still working properly, and I was happy to know that I could still use all my limbs and walk around, even go home later in the day.

At home, my dad immediately gave me a beer and told me to drink up.

"You let me drink now? I mean fuck, why not? I've just been in a coma." I said, taking the beer and chugging it.

"We'll go out drinking tomorrow, how about. You *are* 21…" he said.

"Shit. That's right… All that time wasted just watching TV… I'm so glad I'm not in Hell." I said.

"We kept the TV on sometimes, just so you could have some sounds of life. It felt… awful when we just had to leave you like that. But your mom and I tried to visit when we could…" my dad said.

"You don't have to explain. What day is it, anyway?" I asked.

"All Souls Day. Fitting, that that would be the day that you join us in the living world again…" my dad said, stared at me hard, and poked me. "Just checking if you're not a ghost." he said.

I laughed, and laughed, and laughed, and my dad started laughing too.

My mom just smiled and watched us.

Maggie hugged me close, pressing her breasts up against me, and said, "If you're all alive again, me and my girlfriend are going to the movies."

Dana said, "We're celebrating our two year anniversary. We got together on Halloween, and she just looked… really hot, as that sexy cat."

"I'm her favorite little pussy. See ya… immortal." Maggie said, and Dana and her hugged me again, then left out the door.

I just drank with my parents, talking about all that happened and what has changed.

My mom said, "Do you remember who tried to kill you?"

"Hm… Some old demons of mine… but… I remember a voice… saying to 'Do it quick…' I don't really remember, to be honest. Let's just forget about it. I'll be sure not to get caught like that again." I said.

"We found your knives again… hold onto them, just for yourself." my dad said, and gave me my knives of suffering, kept by my parents.

I put the blades on my belt, and I knew my suffering would continue, for the rest of my life. But that's alright, because that is only called living.

The next day, my dad and I stumbled away from the bar. We were really enjoying the evening, and even if I was the Spawn of Sax, I could never have a better human father. We skipped stones on the lake, and then smoked cigarettes back home.

We saw Mags and Dana holding hands on the porch, making out, but they stopped to greet us and say hello. "It'ssss a shame you didn't catch Maggie when you could've, Paul." my dad said, and hiccupped, "But at leaaast we've all got Dana to reel them in… This chick," and he shook Mags by the shoulder, "is like a second dauuughter to me."

"I'm just glad you don't freak out anymore when Dana and I even just hold hands, Kasey." Mags said.

"Iiii can understand that women want women... I beeeet God is a woman, himself... Women are divinity... so I'm going to go pass out in your mother's arms..." my dad said.

"You just really needed a break, too, Dad." Dana said. My dad smiled, and stumbled inside to my mom.

I talked with Mags and Dana for a bit. Mags whispered in Dana's ear and Dana burst out laughing. "God no, pussycat." Dana said.

"What'd she say?" I asked Dana.

"She... just has a bit of an orgy fetish sometimes. And incest fetish, and every fetish under the sun. It's always a surprise with her... But no, Mags, we're never having a threeway with my brother." Dana said.

Maggie looked around nervously blushing, and I coughed and went inside.

I passed my mom and dad, my dad with his head on my mom's lap as she stroked his hair and looked into her eyes.

I got a call from a number I didn't know, but I knew who it would be.

I answered, and said, "Hi, Tricia."

"...Are you psychic now, too? How did you know my new number?" she said.

"Just a guess. What's up?" I asked.

"...I want you back. I love you. I- I'll break up with him- I love you-" she said.

"You don't have to do that- I mean... I wouldn't want you to give up on someone..." I said.

"...I don't care. All that time, you were dead. And you come back to life, again and again. I want you back, and there's nothing you can do about it. I'm coming over." she said, and hung up.

I let her in, nervous as hell. I've been in Hell for three year, and meeting Tricia, she was like meeting Heaven.

She hugged me, kissed me, and took me to my room. She waved hi to my mom with my dad snoring with his head on her lap.

Tricia and I made love. She stroked my tail, clutched my back, feeling the wings, and she made me feel extra special and nice… like I had really, truly, come back to life.

She was putting back on her clothes, and said, "I'm glad I didn't marry the fucker. I shot him down in an instant… but we still saw each other after…"

"What? You were going to get married?" I said.

"No. I had… a slight sliver of hope for my demon boy." she said, smiled, and kissed me.

I kissed her, and said, "I will never give up on you, either. Even if you leave me, even if you die, I will keep you alive with my love."

She burst out crying, and said, "Tha-That's what I wanted to do for so long… I *wanted* to… But I'm trash… I can't even remain faithful…"

"You've never let me down." I said.

"I've let down others. For you. If you seal this love for me… If you really care… then I will be yours forever." she said.

I kneeled before her… and said, "Then will you marry me, Tricia Antonelli?"

"Yes. You piece of shit demon who can't even remain dead. I love you, you *fucking…* immortal demon boy." she said, we kissed, and made love again.

21

Tricia left in the morning, smiling and kissing me, and I told of my engagement to Tricia to Dana and Mags.

"…You're kidding, right?" Dana said.

"This is like a fucking soap opera or something. I like it." Mags said.

"I just don't want to lose her again, and I don't want her to lose me." I said.

Dana said, "But- marriage is just a ball and chain! It's basically blasphemy to real love! How can you be sure she's not gonna leave you for someone else like she has for you?"

I shrugged, and said, "I don't know. But I've loved her ever since we were little kids."

Mags started a cigarette, and said, "You're still little kids. Just fucking and moaning in love… It's really pathetic. You know you can just pay a woman to be your virtual wife, right? And she'll do it? Just take a test run at that."

"…That sounds really scummy." I said.

"Well, you *are* a demon…" Mags said.

"You know?" I said.

Dana said, "I told her, and then she saw. Freaked her out like crazy the first time, but she actually got used to it pretty fast."

Mags said, "It's hard to fear a demon when they're laying comatose in a bed for years. Tricia and I hang out all the time… She said she really liked this one guy… I'll scope it out for you, just in case."

"You'd do that for me? Not that you have to, or anything. I trust Tricia." I said.

"I just like when the girl gets the guy in the end… and you're our guy… so I hope she gets you." Mags said.

Mags came back later with Tricia, after hanging out with her all day. "You scoping me out?" Tricia said.

"…Uh, I didn't think it was necessary-" I said.

"I'm kidding. I just got rid of that asshole… He didn't even believe me when I sent the text. Fucking scum. He just didn't understand." Tricia said.

"I've never seen such a fight! They were throwing shit left and right! But then she threatened him with her bass, and he got the fuck out of there." Mags said.

"You've got a home now, Paul. Wanna stay with me? I just have to move the crap that reminds me of my ex out to the curb. Maybe you can help?" Tricia said.

"Uh… I mean, if you want-" I started.

"I'll help her. You just chill in the living world for a while, ok?" Mags said.

"Let's get started. See ya, lover." Tricia said, kissed me, and left.

Tricia waved me goodbye, smiling in glee.

I sat on the porch bench with Dana, and we watched them drive off.

Tricia was blowing me kisses from the window.

"So what did you do for her that got her so stuck on you?" Dana asked.

I started a cigarette, and said, "I probably am no one she can count on, I die and leave everyone every fucking time… but I did take away her knife that she was using to cut herself. She's never cut herself after that."

"Yeah… That's nice. You'd think being a demon would drive women away from you instead of attracting them… You've got giant slashes on your face from fighting a demon, wings, a tail, and horns… but still you have to fight them off with a stick." Dana said as I passed her the cigarette.

"Maybe it's kind of like their realization of a dirty romance novel?" I said, as she puffed.

"Haha… Yeah. Help the poor lost suffering demon boy out of Hell and into the gates of Heaven… Into their twat." Dana said.

"I'm glad there's one woman out there who's immune to the fantasy. My best and only sister. How are you with Mags?" I said, and took back the cigarette.

"It's been really nice with her. She's a cool cat, and I don't have to worry about being weird with her, cuz she's the weirdest woman under the sun. It's a breather from finding that perfect match, that lock and key to open your soul and body and yada yada… I can just hang out with my weird, perverted girlfriend and relax. But *man…* She is just never satisfied. All those toys and shit she's got- I mean… She's just got a strong, healthy sexual appetite." Dana said.

"You've lost me there. And I won't speculate." I said

"We're thinking of taking a break… Just so I can explore and she can go wild again. I'm thinking of dating this transsexual at my work… He's just got very pretty eyelashes, and we connect on a lot of stuff." Dana said.

"I suppose two years is a good milestone. I bet you two will get together again after she gets exhausted from love, and you've scouted out the continent." I said.

"I'll always hold my little pussycat close… Even if she gets a thousand STDs and ends up as my virtual wife." Dana said, and smiled.

So, I moved in with Tricia. I was a little nervous, and I really had nothing of real value besides the knives, but Tricia had a TV, a couch, and… a bed. The first place she brought me, and we had a little house-warming party underneath the covers.

We were in the throes of passion, but I heard a noise, the door open, and Maggie was watching us, basically drooling at our naked bodies.

"Goddamnit, what the hell are you doing here?" I said, and Tricia and I stopped lovemaking.

"You need a tag in, Trish?" Mags said.

Tricia was blushing, and said, "I know I gave you a key, but not to my room when we're fucking."

Mags sat on the bed next to us, which just unnerved me more, and she said, "Dana and I are taking a break. Wanna see this hot breakup pic she sent me??" and opened a picture on her phone to show us. I quickly averted my gaze, seeing only briefly my sister posed so erotically…

Tricia said, "Huh. That's a pretty neat outfit."

Mags said, "I got it for her one time… and I hope she keeps it." Mags looked back at the phone and sighed at the picture of Dana, "You two just have that perfect craving… each other. I get cravings for that one bodybuilder in my gym, the librarian who always bends over so nice when she's stacking books… even you two. I envy your relationship. I'm thinking about prostitution."

"What?" I said, "Don't sell yourself. That's just a quick road to danger and death."

"Not *my* prostitution… I mean, maybe… but like, the girls in the city. The courtesans, the gigolos… all in a big brothel, just for me." Mags said.

Tricia said, "We'll take you somewhere that it's legal and you can binge your heart out. Somewhere in Holland or something. That way it's at least safer."

"You'd do that?? Or… y'know, we can just cuddle together… Just for a night? Or I can watch?" Mags said.

Tricia and I looked at each other, frowning. We looked back at her, looking at us so hopeful, and I tried to let her down easy…

"I-I mean… Let's just watch a movie? C'mon, we d-don't have to do anything! Just watch a movie!" she said.

"Alright." Tricia said.

"Cool! Just finish up, and I'll work on the popcorn!" Mags said.

"We're done, Mags." Tricia said.

"Damn. Alright." Mags said.

Tricia and I sat next to each other, but Mags squeezed in the middle of us with a big bowl of popcorn, right in between her legs.

Mags rubbed our thighs as we watched the movie. It kind of startled us, so she wrapped her arms around our shoulders and said, "You two are my best friends, I mean that. Not like that idiot Renley caring for his kid… I invited him over to visit you guys, just so you know."

"You did? You should tell me before you rent out my apartment to old friends." Tricia said.

"I just want to kiss you." Mags said to Tricia.

Tricia got up, as Mags still had her arm around my shoulder, turned to Mags, with her hands on her hips, and said, "Just go jerk it off, Mags. I'm sick of you trying to get into our pants. If you want to be my friend, then I don't want to have to hose you down every time you think of sex. It's just… filthy, inappropriate… and I don't think anyone else would take this if you weren't their friend."

Mags sighed, and said, "Oh… Ok… I-I'm sorry… I thought it would be neat, being alone again… Being tied to one woman, and only one woman, is a bit of a ballbreaker sometimes. I'll hose myself off and take a shower… Can I use yours?"

Tricia smiled and said, "Sure. Take as long as you like." Mags smiled, and went to the bathroom.

We heard her moaning in the shower.

22

I was sleeping with Tricia, and I woke up in a fright of... well, not Hell, but what got me there.

Someone had tried to kill me. Would they try again?

Was it just those demons trying to ruin my life? Or was there something more sinister by what that man said? Do it quick... I tried to go back to sleep, but gave up and crept around the apartment, checking if the windows were sealed, the door locked.

Tricia blinked her eyes open as I was checking if the knives were just in reach of the bed, and she said, "Paul? What's up? It's late."

"Nothing, Tricia. I'm... just worried." I said.

"Nothing will happen to you... It'll be ok." she said, smiling sweetly.

"I'm not really worried about me. I've basically died. I'm worried if they- If they- find you, instead of me... I just don't want that to happen." I said.

She got out of bed, as I was checking the lock on the window, and gave me a hug.

"We'll fly somewhere safe, where no one can hurt us. We'll fly away from all of them." Tricia said.

I hugged her back, and said, "Ok. Do you mind if I just watch TV for a bit? I can't sleep."

"Sure. Come back to bed soon..." she said, and kissed my cheek.

I went to the living room and turned on the TV and all the lights. I guess I just had a fear of the dark these days, and it was nice in light and sound.

Someone knocked on the door.

I instantly wielded my knives, and went to answer. I opened it only on a crack, concealing a knife behind the door.

But it was only Mags.

I let her inside, and it looked like she had been crying. "I-I... I'm so alone..." she said.

I was wary she'd try to hug the crap out of me or fondle me or something, but she just sat on the sofa and tried wiping off the tears.

"What's up, Mags?" I said, sitting beside her.

"D-Dana... is giving me the cold shoulder... I propositioned we just be friends with benefits... but no... she has to put her whole heart and body into a relationship... Makes me feel like trash..." Mags said.

"We don't all have the same appetites as you, Mags..." I said.

"But... Why?? Is it something with how I was raised? I was always told to never have sex until I was married and crap... But you don't need to! You can just fuck anyone you like! As long as you've got confidence in yourself... You feel no shame! None at all!" she said.

"You sound like you're trying to convince yourself, instead of me." I said.

She looked to her feet, and said, "I've been on the pill ever since high school. Never miss a dose. I swear I had herpes before Dana... and I told her, and she took precautions... I-I... I just... am no one anyone really loves... I'm just a sap with breasts..."

"I think you've got a great mind, talents, skills, and all sorts of things. No one can play drums like you, Mags."

"I just don't know what I'm going to say to Renley tomorrow. Good job? You got a girl pregnant? I wonder if that will ever happen to me...

I can't imagine a bigger mistake than having a child with someone you don't love."

"Then just take it easy for a while? Don't have sex for a little bit? You didn't have to worry about getting pregnant with Dana… Maybe just continue the lesbo life if it truly worries you?"

She laughed a bit, and said, "That's fine for a straight person to say. For a bisexual like *me* it gets tough sticking to one sort of love. Bodies, people, love, it's always different, and never the same. I- Can I sleep on the couch? I won't try to interrupt you guys again…."

Tricia was watching her from our bedroom door, and said, "Oh… You poor thing. Just cuddle with me. No funny business, and you can sleep with me."

Mags smiled, and went to bed with Tricia, where they snuggled up. I told them I would be in in a minute.

Two girls in one bed… You'd think I'd rush off to that as soon as I could… but I had to check the lock again…

The next day we met with Renley, and he got a bit plumper, but not too plump. He was always as tall and thin as a stick before, but now he looked a bit well rounded.

And his Spanish girlfriend was… well, she was interesting.

We all had lunch together. We reminisced about the old days and talked to each other about what happened in our lives.

"Chica and I studied as hard as we could before the baby… and we're thinking I can continue some of my studies again when I'm not working to try to give the little Lazarus an even better home with my education." Renley said.

"Lazarus?" I asked, taking a sip of my soda.

"The child. He's just given us a new life, y'know?" Renley said, and smiled.

Chica spoke in Spanish, and Renley spoke in Spanish back to her. Chica said in English to us, "I came to this country for the education. Where I could truly make something of myself... I did not plan to get pregnant so young... But Renley and I just really-"

Renley said quickly, "We just felt the mood was right."

Mags said, "What? In the back alley?"

Chica glared at her, and said, "No. The party was a very nice one, even though-"

Renley said, "We were both drunk and couldn't remember anything but each other..."

We all sat in silence for a second, and Tricia said, "...Good for you. Do you have time to play with us, Renley?"

Renley sighed, and said, "We've got to get back to Lazarus at Chica's mom's house. I actually sold my guitar to have a bigger nest egg for Lazarus... It'd be nice to play again... but maybe we can watch them, Chica?"

Chica and Renley spoke in Spanish to each other, and Chica nodded. "We have enough time for now." she said.

We played, Dana, Mags, Tricia, and I, for Renley and Chica.

They watched, and Renley was tapping his foot at our new song, and Chica had her eyes open in awe. We played a sort of bluesy, jazzy, metal, and I sang to Dana's riffs, Mags's beats, and Tricia's bass.

When it was over, Chica and Renley yelled out "Encore! Encore!" and applauded.

So we rocked some more.

We later hugged them goodbye, and they said they'd love to catch our next show when they could.

They drove off, and Tricia put an arm around my shoulder, saying, "I feel bad for them... but kinda good, y'know?"

"Yeah. They seem like they're really taking this seriously. You think we could really have a real performance?" I said.

Dana and Mags were playing in the garage, but suddenly it seemed to get very quiet.

"I think we should give it a shot. I mean, what else have we got to do but get married? We gotta follow our passions." Tricia said, and we walked into the garage.

With Mags and Dana groping and kissing each other on the couch. "And we should let these two follow theirs. Let's go inside." Tricia said, and we left Mags and Dana to kiss each other.

23

Mags convinced Dana to be "friends with benefits," at least until Dana felt like she needed to put her whole heart into a relationship. I suppose Mags used a lot of convincing, or at least kissed Dana in the right way.

We booked a concert at a coffee shop for a start. Tricia's father and the owner of the coffee shop were friends, and it was a real hip coffee shop with live performances going on all the time.

We decided we'd try to get our name out publicly, and let people know the band name Spawn of Sax. Underground stuff is fine, of course, and we contemplated playing for a few house parties, but if we wanted to do this right we wanted to do so in an open setting where anyone could watch us if they wanted. This performance was really all about seeing if we could pull it off, Tricia and Mags being the only ones of us who've played publicly before, and Tricia only in band in high school.

It was chilly out, and I wore my red scarf as Tricia and I talked, walked, and mentally prepared for our show. "Man, people will think you're one lucky dog, when they see you're the only guy in a band full of chicks…" Tricia said.

I laughed, and said, "I *am* lucky. I'm even going to be spending the rest of my life with one of those chicks."

"I'm glad you think so." Tricia said, holding my hand, "You really make me feel special that I found you like I did. You're magic, and your very first magic trick pulled my heart out of my chest."

I squeezed her hand tight.

We played at the coffee shop, very nervous before we started, but Mags said, "Ok! One, two!" and started the beat, then everything sort of fell into place.

People were cheering for us! They were whooping and dancing! And we continued the everliving music.

Tricia played a bass solo, and then Dana rocked with her and they played a duet, as I stepped back in silence.

I turned back to the crowd and roared! *I let my inner demon shout out to the world!*

Everyone was silent for a second.

And then cheered!

We accepted the applause at the end of the performance. Some people were asking if we sold any albums, and I was saying, "Sorry. No-"

But Tricia said, "Catch our new album next month! The Spawn of Sax's debut album will be out soon!" and smiled to the crowd as they cheered.

I asked Tricia if we could really make an album in just one month, and she said, "Hell yeah!! That was such a rush! I'm going to sell off some extra crap and get some recording equipment. This will be a blast!!"

The four of us sat around the garage and wrote and tried out music. We could cover a few things, but we really wanted to put our own personal touch into our music.

I said, "Ok, I've got something written… Wanna listen to it?" to my band. They nodded, and I began my song.

"It's Christmas in the spring, I'm all out of things to say…

"You make me feel that way, like I'm just an out of luck rocker…

"I want to be there someday, in the sky, where we all can play…

"Rock and roll, metal, jazz and blues…

"Where it's all fine in the news, no one cares what they do…

"We can laugh and sing, caring not about a thing…

"I thank you, for giving me the spring.

"I thank you for everything…

"You're an angel on the wing, with a golden ring…

"As I sing…" I sang.

They listened as I continued. They listened as I sang my first song of thanks to Yule.

Mags started a drum beat, and Dana played guitar. Tricia began on bass, and smiled to me.

When we were done, Tricia said, "That's a sweet way to think of her."

I smiled, and said that Yule saved my life.

Tricia said, "I'm glad she did. I would never have you without her. Well! That's one song down, let's think of the next!" And we continued our practice.

We soon had recorded a good eight songs album. Then we began to sell.

The street corner was a bit difficult to catch people's attention on, but it was the busiest corner in town, and we played music and passed out albums for people to listen to. We accepted a few donations from people, but mostly we gave the copies out for free.

Until the cops came in and told us it was illegal to assemble like this…

Mags was about to say something cutting to Dave the cop, but I said, "We'll get out of here as soon as we pack up. Want to take an album with you? Maybe you can play it at the station or in your car if you get bored of the police scanner."

Dave laughed, and said, "Sure. And I want to let you know… We haven't forgotten about you, Paul. Just so you know."

I asked him what he meant.

"There's someone out there who tried to kill a kid like you. We'll keep an eye out for the Spawn of Sax in the future." Dave said, winked, got in his car with his partner and drove off with a copy of our album.

We played at multiple places, bars, coffee shops, and soon... put together a concert in the park.

We rocked and rolled! We played our jazzy, bluesy, metal, and people were really having a good time.

Except for one person. A man with one arm who approached us after we played our final song, my song of thanks to Yule for saving my life.

Yule screamed out, and actually tried to fly across the crowd to the man.

But the one armed man pointed a gun at us.

And shot Tricia Antonelli, the woman I love.

I looked at her falling. It felt like I was in slow motion. I couldn't conceive what was happening, as she fell to the stage floor, bleeding from her forehead.

I screamed out a demonic roar.

Everyone saw what I was.

My horns, which I had been filing down to nothing, erupted from my head into jagged spikes, twisting and curling across my head.

My claws, ripping through the flashy gloves and boots I wore for the occasion.

My spiked tail, flicking back and forth in my anger.

I flew at the man, tackling him as he smiled.

I slashed at his throat with my knives, which I carried with me, *always*.

He was still smiling as he bled out on the grassy park ground.

"*I* did it quick... Now you will know what it's like... to want what you once had..." the man croaked out, and died.

People were screaming, running, and police cars and ambulances rushed to the scene. Yule was kneeling before Tricia, and as I looked at Yule's expression and Tricia's body, I knew that Tricia was dead.

I picked up Tricia's body, and flew away with her. Yule flapped after me, as I screamed in despair.

Part 5: Avaritia

Greed

24

I didn't know where to go. I just stared down at Tricia's lifeless eyes, held her still body in my arms… and I kept flying up.

"Paul! We need to go back!" Yule yelled out to me as I kept ascending.

"No! I'll take her to Heaven myself!! I will!!" I yelled back.

"She'll get there with help from others now… Just come back with me, please!" Yule said.

"I'm going to join her there! We'll never be separated again!" I yelled.

Yule flew before me, and stared calmly into my eyes. She said it will be alright, and we needed to do Tricia's body justice.

I stared back into her eyes, as Yule looked at me sadly, and I bawled my eyes out. I flapped down to the Earth with her, enveloped in my sadness.

Tricia was gone.

All that time she had been witness to me coming back to life over and over… all that time she had waited for me, come back to me… but there was no way to bring her back when she had died.

Yule said she would take care of her body, and told me to go home. "But-" I started.

"Go home, Paul. You're going to have to deal with a lot of shit soon, people, police, wanting to talk to you. Just rest easy for the night."

I slowly released Tricia into Yule's arms, and walked back home.

Satan, Stan, the Devil, was waiting in the shadows for me.

I swore at him! I yelled at this awful creature!

He started a cigarette, and whispered, *"All you needed was to be put on the path... and you found your own way to Hell on Earth. Every time, I have helped you, aided you. I gave you a love, when you were scorned by Tricia. I gave you a weapon to protect yourself. I protected you from the law as a murderer. And I even kept you alive, after you refused to repay me for my kindness. Everything you did was your own justice... because you were greedy with this life, you wanted more and more... and could never stop. You, and Tricia, got what you deserved..."*

"Go back to Hell, monster." I said.

He smiled at me, and said he'll join me there soon.

When I slice my own wrists.

I blinked, and he was gone.

I stared at the knives when I got home. It would be so easy. Just slice, and then sleep. I could be gone, and maybe, just maybe, I'd be with Tricia again.

I held the knife over my wrist. I could do it, I assured myself. I could have that chance to be with Tricia again.

But someone let themselves in Tricia's... and my apartment. I looked around the corner, and Mags and Dana were crying.

They went up to me, hugging me, and I dropped the knives to the floor.

I hugged both of them tight.

In the next few days I spent a long time talking to police officers and the like. I was tired and frustrated with them near the end, which only made them tug on me all the more.

But soon enough it was over. They wanted to ask me more questions soon, they said.

I called Renley up and told him about Tricia.

"...I'm so sorry." he said, "Listen... Whatever happens, don't do anything rash. I know it's tough losing someone... but..."

"But what? Tricia's dead!! She's... fucking gone..."

"Just keep a calm head. If you ever need to talk, let me know, ok?"

I said ok, and hung up.

I wanted to talk to Tricia. I wanted to talk to God, and demand that he give her back.

But instead of talking to God, I talked to Yule.

She was a forty two year old woman, with her forty two year old husband. I thought of her as an aunt.

But I knew she was an angel from Heaven, and I yelled at her, screamed at her, asking her why she couldn't have done anything.

"I... I'm sorry, Paul. I did all I could. I gave Tricia peace in death." Yule said sadly.

"What?! The fuck is that going to do!!" I yelled.

"She... wanted to give you this." Yule said.

Yule got up from sitting, and lit her white flame in her hand. I nervously stared at it as she touched it lightly to my forehead.

I saw Tricia. I felt all of our happy memories together. I felt sadness. She wanted to say sorry.

She showed me the memories of the other people she spent time with, forgetting about me even for a while, abandoning me. She even told a few of them she loved them, in an effort to try and forget me.

She showed me the memory of me proposing to her, and I could feel that that was the happiest moment in her life.

I felt her lips on my lips, as she kissed me goodbye. I didn't want to let her go.

I felt her being lifted up and away from me, ascending.

I reached out to grab at her... but she passed through my fingers, and I knew she was gone.

I collapsed to kneeling, the tears falling from my face.

25

I drank alone at the bar. I found a different way to mourn Tricia, just get as drunk as possible. It felt like she was near me, in a way, when I couldn't even feel my body.

Somebody was picking on me, some drunk asshole I used to know from high school. I turned to him, and asked him if he wanted to play poker. He laughed, and said I was going to lose everything to him.

We played, and even though he cheated the entire time… it was only human cheating. Nothing close to that of a demon's tricks.

He was sweating, as I bet all of his cash I won, his golden watch, even an erotic picture of his girlfriend. I bet it all to give him one last chance. He said he didn't have anything else to wager.

The bar got dark, the people around us could not be seen or heard.

I lit my red, demonic flame in my hand, a trick I tried to learn from the Devil, but I could've only learned from Yule, just by watching closely.

I said, in a cold, hollow, and *demonic* voice, *"You have your soul. How about that? Win, and you will have everything and more back to you. Lose, and you are mine."*

He stared around at the darkness, and said, "A-Are you really the spawn of the Devil??"

I smiled, and said, *"No. I'm the Spawn of Sax."*

He slowly nodded.

I revealed my hand, putting a card down one by one with my clawed hands.

He gulped, and dropped his cards to the table. He had four kings.

And I had five kings.

There's always a better cheater somewhere.

"I am the son of the King of Hell. Your soul is now mine." I said.

"B-But you cheated!!" he said.

I smiled, and said, "As did you, in every hand. You couldn't see my tricks over your greed. But I will be lenient towards you. I will simply take a piece of your soul. *Don't worry. You won't miss it."*

A piece of his own bright flame of a soul came out of his chest, and was added to the dark red flame in my hand.

He was gasping for breath, and I left his possessions on the table and walked out the door.

I smoked a cigarette on my walk home, lighting it with my flame... with the very piece of soul I just added to my collection.

I had been gathering bits and pieces from random people, little scraps here and there... mostly the things people wanted to get rid of. One person didn't want that part of him that loved chocolates so much, so I took it. Another wanted to stop cheating on his wife, so I added it to my flame. This guy... just needed to stop being such an asshole. I mean, who bets their soul over pocket change, a watch, and a naked picture?

The next day I saw Tricia again. The funeral for Tricia was fine. Just fine. People still looked at me oddly, some remembering that they think they saw me become a demon and fly off... but I hung around with Dana and Mags most of the time, as they knew Tricia the best as friends besides me, and the two sort of smoothed over any lingering fear people had of me.

I said a few words for my once fiancée, and later talked to Tricia's father alone.

He stared at me for a second at the table. His wife, kids, and father were busy mourning and talking to others.

He said, "I didn't think anything crazy like this would happen again… I didn't think- I'd lose my oldest child so young…" and looked at me sadly, "But she was always crazy about you… Said something about how you saved her life… What did she mean?"

I took out one of the knives, Tricia's knife, and placed it on the table. I could only tell it was Tricia's because mine had a slight notch on the cross, and Tricia's was pristine.

"Ah." he said, "That knife. It came from my grandfather who fought in World War 2. I don't have a clue where he got it. It always was a skeleton in my closet… but as it helped keep him alive in the past, my father wanted to keep his memory alive with it, and so did I. And I wanted it to help keep Tricia alive…"

"You can have it back if you want. It's only a tool, and Tricia didn't know how to use it properly. It hurt her, instead of help her." I said.

"No… No, thank you… I can only imagine how much she suffered with it… Hold onto it, for her. I just- I just miss her so much…" Mike, Tricia's father, said, and put his hands to his face.

I lit my flame slightly in my hand. I could take away this man's pain… I could take away his grief for the loss of his daughter.

I stared at him crying into his hands, and started reaching to him with the flame.

But then I stopped, and extinguished my flame.

Let him keep his grief and suffering. Let him remember how much Tricia meant to all of us.

Later in the day, Mags and I were hanging out, just drinking at the bar. Dana had found another match, and Mags was alone again, but assured that they would get back together when Dana found some insignificant flaw in her search for a perfect romance. Mags and I drank, we laughed…

Then she said something that reminded me so very much of Tricia.

I looked deep into her eyes, as she looked into mine.

We kissed each other.

A long, deep kiss… tongues flirting as we embraced…

Then we broke off.

We walked home, and I… I couldn't stop holding her hand, like I had done with Tricia so many times.

We were trying to watch TV together, just to enjoy each other's company. We had told each other sorry over and over again, saying it wouldn't happen again.

But she attacked me with her beautiful body on the couch, wrapping me up with her.

I wrapped my tail around her, keeping her in my embrace.

She moaned out as I did as well, and we continued in our passion.

When we were done, she was making coffee, actually running to the coffee machine as she was nude, and I was putting back on my clothes, ashamed.

She said, "D-Do you want to see the r-rest of the movie? What were we watching again?"

I looked back at the TV. I don't know what the heck it was. I said I needed to take a walk.

I walked out the door quickly, and then noticed I had forgotten my shoes.

I don't think I could've gone back for them, not with… not with Mags there.

I walked and lit a cigarette in my pocket, an old crumpled one but still usable, with my flame.

I looked at the souls, admiring each of their perfect flaws. It was only pieces of people, just parts… but altogether, it looked like it could be a person, maybe.

It was me. I had absorbed all of these people, their little bits and pieces, and they were all me. Everyone I had come into contact with had been incorporated… and I believed I would take their pieces to Heaven…

Or destroy them in Hell.

I found a dollar on the street, and I pocketed it.

I kept walking, enjoying the night air and solitude. I thought Tricia would like a night walk if she could…

I sighed, knowing that I betrayed her. I betrayed her memory.

I sighed again, and walked back home, passing the homeless prostitute on the corner.

I gave her the dollar, and she croaked in a raspy voice, "For free? You don't want anything?"

"I'll take something. Just a bit." I said.

"Ok. You better give me more than a dollar… Let's go, sweetheart…" she said, and grabbed my hand.

"Not that. Just a bit of you…" I said, and I grabbed the piece of soul in her chest that loved crack so much.

She was gasping for breath after I had taken the piece of her flame, and she dropped her crack pipe to the street where it fell down a storm drain.

I walked back home, with my new piece of soul. I wonder what crack would feel like?

I got back home and Mags was gone.

She left me a note, saying, "I love you."

I incinerated the note with my flame.

I went to bed.

26

I ignored Mags's call in the morning, and the next around noon. Instead, I went to Tricia's grave.

I was very drunk.

I placed the flowers on her grave, and poured the rest of my beer on the ground for her.

I stumbled to Yule's house, and knocked on her door. She opened, and asked me, "You feeling alright? You look like you had a little too much to drink."

I mumbled, "I'm fine! I'm always... I'm feeling awful."

She invited me inside, and her cat mewled up to me. He looked just like Yule's old cat...

I swore he just said something when my back was turned. He had sworn under his breath at me.

I turned to the cat. He was just licking his paw.

Yule and I talked, and she consoled my grievances. But she got a call from a friend of hers, an old man who was getting sick. He said he really wanted to see Yule again. Yule said to me, "I... I have to go. Do you want to meet my friend with me?"

I shrugged in drunkenness, and nodded, walking out the door with her. The cat said, "Give Thaniel a big steak on me, Yule."

I turned back at the cat quickly, but he was just sleeping with his eyes closed. I rubbed my eyes and went with Yule.

We got to this quaint house where this man lived alone most of the time, but it had three cars pulled up to it, and I walked up the steps with Yule. A woman who looked a little bit older than me opened up, and hugged Yule immediately. She introduced herself to me as Julia.

We got to the bedroom where two men, two brothers, were arguing with the old man, their father sick in bed.

The old man said, "You know it won't hurt too much! And if it does… I'll just drink the pain away!"

The younger brother said, "No, Dad. Drinking is what got you into this mess. If you weren't such an idiot drunk you would be skipping around like a young man."

The dad said, "Skipping? Your mother make you into some sort of sissy? I'm a real man! I can take anything! See, I'll show you!" and he tried to get up from the bed quickly, but clutched at his chest and laid back down. Julia went up to him quickly, and tucked him back in.

The older brother said, "Your heart isn't strong enough, Dad. Can you *please* go to the hospital with us?"

The dad said, "Bah… What are they goin' to do? Drug me up with so much anesthesia I'd feel like I'm dead already? Then they'll give me the bill and I'll wish I was!"

Julia said, "We just want you to be safe and healthy, Dad."

"Fuck it, I've got you all here… I feel fine! And Yule will take the pain away! I know it! I mean look at her! She's a goddamn angel! Heya, Yule. Can you help me?" the dad said, grinning.

Yule said, "I can drive you to the hospital, if you like, Thaniel."

Thaniel's grin left, and he grumbled. "Fuckin'… Fine. If even you think I should go, then I will. But the chest pains don't last too long, anyway…

Who's the dude with the sad look on his face? *He* makes me wish I had pains, just so I could focus on something else besides his sad mug..."

Yule said, "This is Paul, a friend of mine."

I shook Thaniel's hand, and he smiled. I couldn't help but smile back. "Knew a kid like you wasn't such a bummer all the time... Well, help me up, Jule, and let's go..." Thaniel said, and Julia helped her father up and to the car.

Thaniel moaned the whole time, and cursed at his dead father for giving him a heart disease.

Thaniel told me to check out his book before we left him at the hospital, with his three children all looking after him there. I wondered if the Bees of Ferdinand was any good?

I got back to Yule's house with her, and when we opened up the door Max had come back home. I could've sworn he was arguing with someone, but when we got in there was no one there but the cat and Max.

Max said to Yule, "Will Thaniel be ok?"

Yule said, "He shouldn't have too much trouble with the meds they're putting him on. He just thought it was some normal ache or pain... but his heart trouble is increasing. Julia said that it looked like he had a cardiac arrest almost one time. They called in an ambulance, but Thaniel still had enough fight in him to hold them off."

"Man... That sucks. I know that having heart pains is absolutely horrible. He should be fine, but goddamn Rasputin thinks-" Max said.

"Rasputin?" I said.

"Uh... Anyway, I just got a new car to fix up! Want to check it out, guys?" Max said.

I said I wasn't feeling too good... Death was on my mind. So Max threw me a bag of chips, understanding sadly, and told me to just watch TV for a bit. Yule and him went to his new car, I sat on the sofa, and the cat sat on my lap.

I pet him as he purred.

I said to him, "You're a good cat. You're lucky, you've got nine lives to live through… Tricia only had one."

He continued purring, and I continued.

I said, "She was the best gal in the world… And I- I lost her… She probably wouldn't want me back now… I had sex with her best friend. I feel like I really am an awful demon…"

The cat mewled at me.

I said, "It was… It was good. I hate that it was. But it felt- It felt like I was with Tricia, in a way… It felt like- It felt comfortable."

The cat cleaned his ear with his paw.

"But I betrayed her, in death, and there's no way to say I'm sorry." I said.

The cat said, "Dying sucks."

I jumped off the couch, scattering the cat from my lap.

The cat said, "Hey now, I was just getting comfortable."

"What- What the fuck?" I said.

"Oh, just get over it. Didn't you know cats are as smart as they look?" the cat said.

"Are you some sort of demon?" I asked him.

"Are you?" he said.

"Uh… I don't know." I said.

"Well that makes you pretty stupid. You look like a demon to me." he said.

"You look like a cat." I said.

"And thus I am." he said.

"I don't trust you." I said, lighting my flame and threatening the cat.

The cat just stared at me and yawned. He said, "I think I've had that death before. Dying by fire. Although, I've never died from a demon's fire. Honestly I don't think that's possible, as you are only a figment of the writer's imagination."

I tried to hold the flame up and look intimidating, but it didn't seem to scare the cat.

So I said, "I think you're a figment of my imagination."

"And thus I am." he said.

"Ok. Then I just am grieving too much and drinking too much, and now I'm hearing voices..." I said, "It's some sort of PTSD."

"That could happen." the cat said.

"Is this what pushes me over the edge? A talking cat?" I said.

"I think you've been far over the edge for a long time. Murder, suicide, rape... You live a dark life, Paul." the cat said.

"You know who I am?" I asked.

"I just picked up bits and pieces here and there." he said.

I looked at the flame with the bits and pieces... all the dark parts of people that people didn't want... all the crap that people didn't like about themselves... and they were all swirling around in me.

I was consumed in looking at them, this evil in my soul. I just kept on staring at it.

The cat said, "The harder you hold onto that flame, the more it burns you. Like that Tricia or something."

"What?? I can never let go of Tricia! I promised her my life, as she promised me hers!! And... I'm the reason she died! Georgia's husband wanted me to suffer!! And he killed her. It's my fault... I can never let that go..." I said.

"I wonder how strongly you will be able to hold onto that shame, that grief, that failure. You could, for a long, long time... But life is not so difficult to get accustomed to. It sort of... blows away the pain, the longer you live it." the cat said.

"How would you know what it's like to live a real life... You're just a cat!" I said.

"I know how to die, thus I know how to live. When you don't grasp onto your demise so hard, when you learn to accept it, you also learn how to accept living as well." he said.

I paced back and forth, as the cat watched me. I said, "But Tricia- She couldn't- She wasn't able to-"

The cat said, "It's finito, Paul. You not only have to accept your death, but the deaths of others. These things happen in real life, to real people. People die. And they don't come back. You could see them in the after-life… maybe… but while they live, you can only cherish them, and accept their mortality."

"What are you yakking about? To real people? You sound like you're trying to be a minister." I asked the cat, stopping my pacing.

"Oh. I was just trying to leave a positive message. Am I getting too preachy? Sorry." the cat said, and jumped on a chair, cuddling up on it.

I ate the chips and watched the cat. He was just licking his butt. But his voice seemed to have passed.

Yule and Max came back inside, their hands all covered in oil. "This is going to be a fun one, Max." Yule said.

"I know! I can actually work on it, since it's so old. It's not some fancy new car with all their electric crap… I mean, yeah, electric cars are great, they save the environment and are cheap to use… but they're just not as *fun!*" Max said.

"Feeling better yet, Paul?" Yule asked me.

"I don't know. I've just been talking to your cat." I said.

They laughed, and Yule said, "He's quite a conversationalist, isn't he? And he's so cute! C'mere, little Rasputin! Mewl, mewl, mewl!" Yule said, picked up the cat, and cuddled him in her arms.

Rasputin rolled his eyes.

Yule didn't seem to notice, and was kissing him on the head.

I said I needed to go, I needed to let things go.

I said to Rasputin, "You're not the Devil. You're not God. You may be a cat. But you are a good talker."

Rasputin said, "And thus I am."

I walked out the door.

27

I did something I usually never did, not since I was a kid. I went to church. I prayed alone in the chapel, and I lit my flame before the statue of Jesus.

I said sorry for all these bits and pieces I was carrying, these pieces of souls I stole.

I said sorry to Tricia. I don't know if she heard me.

I tried to say that it would never happen again… that I'd remain faithful to her 'til I die… That I'd kill myself just to relieve these feelings-

But…

I felt a feeling of peace in the chapel, and I listened to the silence. I let go of all my tension, all my pain, all my suffering. I let it go, and looked down at the flame in my palms.

I offered these pieces of souls to God.

And I let them go.

The dark red flame burst apart, scattering into millions of pieces. Little red flames that flew around and around me, enveloping me in an inferno.

Someone opened the door of the chapel, and the flames rushed out the door.

I looked back to see Tricia, what looked like Tricia in the blinding light of the outside, but what turned out to be Maggie.

She said, "Oh! I didn't know you were here. I seem to be the only one who comes here these days. It's weird thinking a demon can just roam around church like this."

She sat beside me and I smiled to her halfheartedly.

"Listen." she said, "I know- that what we did should've never happened... I know that. You probably think I'm just some slut who took advantage of you... but... I just felt sad, honestly, and you make me feel happy."

"I don't think you're any sort of slut. I should've been thinking straight... I've been drinking non stop since Tricia died." I said.

"Yeah, I noticed. Were you praying for her?" Mags asked.

"Yeah..." I said.

We sat in silence for a second, and Maggie knelt down and said a Hail Mary, then said, "Thank you, for giving us Tricia."

"What? But she's gone." I said.

She said, "I think it's better to thank God for a life someone had, instead of yelling at him for taking it away."

I said, "Thank you."

She smiled, sitting back down, and said, "I didn't usually do this... go praying. But I just really needed some extra support from... *anyone.* Tricia and I were best pals, and losing her... it just sucks. I only know the Hail Mary because I looked it up on the internet and memorized it. Thank God it's so short."

I smiled to her, and she smiled back. I looked into her eyes... and I thought I could see the bright white flame in her, her soul reaching out to me, comforting me.

I looked at the flame in my hand. It was pure white.

I tentatively reached out my hand with the flame to Maggie... and she grabbed my hand with my flame. We held hands.

We sat for a long time like that, just in silence, as our souls danced back and forth with each other.

We walked out the doors, and I asked her what that note she left in my apartment was about.

"…I just want you to know you are loved. People love you, I love you. Even though what happened to Tricia was horrible… we all still love you." Maggie said.

"…Thank you, Mags." I said.

I hugged Mags goodbye, and went back home.

A few days later, I was drinking at the bar again, a lot less than what I usually drank, and the drunk asshole came stumbling out of the bathroom and noticed me.

He yelled out to me, "I want it back! Give it back to me!!"

I turned my head to him. He looked clean shaven, smelled nice… and he wasn't looking at me in fury, but more of desperation.

I said, "Want what back, Dylan?"

"Th-That piece of me! Th-That thing you took! Give it back to me!!" he said.

I said, "Want a beer?"

He slowly sat beside me, and I ordered him a beer. He sipped at it, as I was doing to my own.

He politely said, "M-My girlfriend broke up with me… She called me a wuss. I know you did it. I know."

"Maybe that's for the best?" I said.

"But you saw her! She was hot!! She was the sexiest broad in the world! I'm lost without her!! I haven't been able to steal- I mean I haven't been able to cheat- I mean I haven't been able to lie. I know you did it!" he said.

"Why can't you lie?"

"…It feels bad."

"That's all? Come on, say something nice, then, and then I'll know you're lying… because I know you, Dylan…" I said, sipping my beer.

"You're not the spawn of the Devil, and I'm sorry I called you one. You seem like a good person, even though you scare the crap out of me… and I wish I wasn't such an asshole to you. Did it work?"

"Nah. I think you just gave me a compliment and said sorry."

"Shit!! I don't want to be a wuss forever! C'mon! Fight me or something!! I want to have a reason to beat the crap out of you!"

"You don't already? I gave that piece to someone else. I think it's in good hands now."

"…You gave my soul to the Devil. I knew it. Well, get ready! I'm gonna… I'm gonna… drink my drink…" he said, and slurped down his beer and, looking very depressed.

"No. I gave it to the man upstairs."

He spilled his beer, and said, "Huh?"

"I gave your soul to God. Probably why you're being so nice."

"…But I don't believe in God…"

I shrugged.

Dylan and I played Go Fish at a table, and he kept on looking at the picture of his ex girlfriend, with her big, perfect, naked breasts.

I was chatting with Dylan on my walk home. He actually didn't seem like such an asshole.

The Devil was warily creeping around us in the shadows, but I ignored him.

Dylan told me about the electric guitar he got, and told me he was practicing.

I said, "Shit. That's awesome. My sister plays guitar. She just moved to the big city to finish her education… It sucked for her ex girlfriend, but I think they'll both be fine. My sister is selling hotdogs now, but says she's having the time of her life."

"Girlfriend? Girls and girls? She, like, some LGBTQ girl?" he asked.

"I don't really know. I think she just has a lot of expectations for love. She can never find that perfect match, and actually seems to do better in love when she doesn't try too hard."

I invited Dylan inside, and we drank beer and talked in the kitchen. I noticed Mags was still sleeping on my couch.

She just slept here sometimes, we didn't do anything with each other, but we still felt better being in each other's company. Dylan opened his eyes wide at her, and said, "Damn. Is that your girl? She's, like, a perfect 20."

I laughed, and said she was just a friend.

Dylan looked at the picture of the naked girl that he once was fond of, and then threw it in the trash. "There are other fish in the sea." Dylan said.

Part 6: Superbia

Pride

28

I laughed as I was talking to Renley over the phone. He said little Lazarus is growing up so fast...

Dylan, Mags and I went to bars, again and again. Time had passed since Tricia passed, and Mags and I... were growing close.

She told me confidentially she would just have a one night stand and then skip town with guys... It's what she did for a while when she first came back to our small town and before she got together with Dana.

But she and I decided we'd like to try our hand at dating again, so went out with each other.

Dylan was usually a third wheel, but we tried over and over to get him a match. He just... was too nice! No matter how much we each amped him up, put a good word in for him with girls... they'd just see he was the nicest person in the world. I suppose he really had changed from being such an asshole, like how he was for most of his life.

Dylan, Mags and I just played music together, rocking in my parents' garage.

Mags called up Dana, and she agreed to visit for a spell.

When she got home for the weekend, her and Mags immediately went to each other and gave each other a long hug.

Then Dana tried to kiss Mags, but Mags turned her head and Dana's lips hit Mags's cheek instead.

Dana looked surprised, and said, "Huh. I guess you are taking it seriously with my brother. Ok."

Mags smiled nervously, and said, "Paul and I only kissed once or twice... and those were just when we were each going home, and didn't know how to say goodbye properly..."

Dana laughed uproariously, and asked who was the wuss in the corner of the room.

Dylan smiled weakly, and said, "That's what I get for having my soul stolen by the Spawn of Sax..."

Dana said, "Ah. Well, I think you're pretty cute. Tell me... what kind of music do you like? What's your favorite food?"

Dylan said, "Um. I do like cheese curds."

"Cheese curds? Strange answer... Unique. Ever been to the county fair? They have all sorts of great things there. What do you think about..." Dana said, continuing grilling Dylan to see if he fits her perfect match.

We all just hung out and talked. Dana was surprised mostly at Dylan's remarks. It seemed that whatever Dana expected Dylan to say, he would say something that was completely off her frame of reference. Dana expected him to either be to one side or the other, too extreme or not enough, but Dylan seemed to fit right in... the perfect center.

And they both loved guitar.

They played in the garage, twisting the amp up to the max, and danced around each other as they tried to outdo each other's playing.

Mags and I just sat and watched. I had never seen Dylan, or Dana, rock so hard.

They were sweating, and it seemed neither of them was going to win at their rock and roll. They both were missing notes.

"Draw?" Dana said.

"Draw." Dylan said.

They sat on the chairs and we talked some more.

Then someone whispered in my ear, someone who's not even supposed to be here… to not even be heard…

"You must be proud of your little family and friends. You must be happy.

"But you'll always be a demon, Saul, the Spawn of Sax.

" I killed Tricia. I killed her by using you.

"You must be proud."

I ignored Satan's evil comments, and focused on my family and friends.

But I knew… I was a demon. I did not belong here.

And neither did Satan.

I soon was pacing back and forth in the living room of Yule's home with Yule sitting on the couch. Rasputin was laying on the table.

"I need to get rid of them. I need to take them all back to Hell… They cause evil with every breath they make on Earth. I need to take my kin back home." I said.

Yule said, "How? By killing them? You would really commit a genocide on all demons?"

"Would you? If they killed someone you love? If they twisted your life, contorting it and controlling it, and used you like a pawn?" I said.

"…I'd want vengeance, yes. How would you even find all of them? Not many people can see through a demon's illusions. I'd say only I can because I came back directly from the afterlife. Some people, true mortals, have learned how to see through demons' tricks, at least partially. You know all these tricks yourself." Yule said.

"There must be some way to take them back… Some sort of magic spell? A religious chant?" I said.

"Demons are drawn to suffering and evil. We could lure them with some sort of event… but it would have to be just such a horrible event that we would be harming instead of helping…" Yule said.

Rasputin said, "Why not ask your father?"

"My father?" I said, "Yeah… Sax. He didn't let them go back to Hell. He left them here… I wonder why…"

So, on that day I went running with Mags on and off, ate a full course meal for every meal, and was exhausted when I finally went to bed.

And I let myself dream.

I dreamed I was in Hell with Sax.

Wait… This wasn't Hell. Sax was here, but there were fluffy white clouds everywhere, and we were in the sky in front of a large gate.

Sax looked quite fit. So fit, he looked like a human.

"Dang! I didn't expect Purgatory to be such a workout!" Sax said to the gatekeeper, flexing his biceps and then running in place. His clothes looked way too big for his human frame.

"I didn't expect you to actually get through the physical parts. You must be proud." St. Peter said to Sax.

"I am! I did a good job! I'm so happy. Well, I'm back off to work… I'll see you later, I guess." Sax said, turning his back to St. Peter.

But St. Peter rested a hand gently on Sax's shoulder, and said, "You've worked long enough, dear soul."

Sax turned back to St. Peter, and said, "What do you mean?"

I walked up to them, and said, "Sax! I need your help taking the demons back to Hell! You're the King of Hell, you have to be able to do something!"

Sax looked at me, and said, "Heya, spawn! I think I did all I could for them… I had this whole royal banquet set up for them! But they were like, 'Oh nooo… He probably poisoned the turkey… Oh nooo… He thinks he's so great, calling himself King of Hell…' It was quite a bummer having to throw out all that extra food."

"What? You invited them back?" I said.

"Invited them to go to Hell, yes. I can see why they refused." Sax said.

"…So… They're all just running amuck through their own free will? St. Peter! Can't God do something?" I said.

St. Peter smiled, and said, "God... is in all of us. Every person, demon or angel. God worked through me, through Yule, through you. I can't believe one angel of war I helped sneak out of Heaven could do so much good... Actually, I did believe it. And now we have you."

"Me?" I said.

"You, Paul." he said.

Sax said, "And me! I'm the King of Hell! I still have so much to amend! I gotta make this shithead's life perfect for screwing him up in the first place and giving him life! I'll go back to Hell and we can plan on kidnapping all the demons and taking them back-"

St. Peter just shook his head slowly, and said, "I think the title of King of Hell belongs to another."

"...Oh." Sax said.

"Be at peace, Paul. You will find the answers you seek." St. Peter said.

I woke up, gently, calmly, peacefully.

And I screamed out in frustration.

Could no one do anything??

Was it always up to me?

I walked out to the streets in the night, knowing what I must do. I walked down the street, alone, looking for Satan, to kill him.

I yelled out, "I'm going to kill you, Satan! I'm going to end you! I'm going to bring you back to HELL!!"

I did not know he was looking for me, instead.

I saw him come out of the shadows and point the gun at me.

"It's time to get what you deserve, Saul. It's time to go to your rightful place... If you will not kill yourself, then I will kill you."

I was sweating, as he aimed the pistol right in between my eyes.

"Y-You can't do it. You've never killed me yet." I said, wielding my knives.

"There's a first time for everything... and I think you're getting far too troublesome. I do enjoy tormenting you... but now you're talking about bringing us all back to Hell... I think I can do the same for you.

"I'm going to kill this world, Saul. I'm going to kill everyone in it.

"And bring their eternal souls to Hell with me.

"Now, RUN. RUN, SPAWN OF SAX."

He laughed and shot bullets at me.

I ran.

He chased me through the streets, through alleys and ditches, through a graveyard eventually.

I tried to cloak myself in shadow, I tried to shield myself from the Devil's sight.

But he saw through every illusion of mine, he saw me.

Whenever I blinked, he would be before me behind a gravestone, aiming the gun at me.

Whenever I turned a corner, he was waiting and about to shoot.

Whenever I ran, I felt him chasing me, faster than I could move my feet.

I told myself to wake up. I told myself this must be a dream. This must be the worst nightmare ever.

But I knew that the Devil was actually chasing me, like a lion who just got tired of ripping a sheep to pieces, keeping it alive, and wished to enjoy the meal fully now.

I prayed to God! I prayed to Yule! I prayed to anyone!!

I saw my saving grace. A yellow car stopped on the curb outside of the graveyard gates.

Thank God.

Dylan picked me up, and I told him to drive as fast as he could.

I looked back at the Devil on the curb as we raced away. He pointed his pistol at me...

I knew he wouldn't miss.

But I saw him grin, and put his pistol back in his holster.

"Holy shit!!" Dylan said, "Who was that guy?? I- I- felt like my life was about to end when I saw him!!"

"You're telling me. That was the Devil, Dylan." I said. Dylan gulped, and drove a bit faster.

29

Dylan dropped me off at Mags's place, and went to take off early tonight... just so he could be safe at home, and not on the dangerous streets...

I knocked on her door, still panting from my escape from the Devil.

She opened up, smiling, as I looked around nervously, and she brought me inside.

She was chatting like she usually did, but I tried as hard as I could to listen to her. I had gotten a lot better at keeping up with her momentum of words.

I heard a noise by the window, and rushed to it with my knives, peeking out the window.

I saw a family of raccoons rush out of the bushes and scamper down the street.

"...You feeling ok?" Mags said.

"No. The archnemesis of creation just tried to murder me." I said.

"Oh. That... That one guy you told me about? Th-The Devil?"

"Yes. And he threatened the entire world with death as well."

"Um. Ok... How do we stop that?"

"I don't know. Fight back. Kill him before he kills us." I said, still looking hard at the bushes.

"Just watch TV for a bit. It'll all work out… Yeah…" Mags said, and went to her room.

I watched TV, relaxing as I saw Bugs Bunny outwit the Tasmanian Devil.

I could outwit him. I could beat Satan. I hoped I could.

Mags came back with a box of stuff and sat on the couch next to me.

I looked at the stuff, then did a double take.

"This one… We had some good times." she said, and cracked the short whip.

"Huh? Doing some cleaning?" I said.

"Sorta. I figured I am going to keep only one of them, besides the fantastic little vibrator. I really don't need them as much as I did, and they've been kind of embarrassing to keep around." Mags said, rummaging around in her box of sex toys.

She showed me the handcuffs, and said, "Oohlala. We can play dirty cop one last time, if you like."

"Um. I really hate being bound. Just reminds me of that time the Devil nearly killed me before…" I said.

She took out the strap on, attached it to herself and danced around with her giant plastic dick. She said, "Dana loved this one. You ever think of being pegged?"

"…No." I said.

She sat back down, and took out a riding crop. She sighed, and said, "I do wish I could fuck TNK with this…"

"Who's that?" I said.

"Just a character from this book I've been reading. It's fun to role-play." she said, and gasped, and brought out some garments, sexy bits of underwear. She said, "My first pieces of lingerie… I had forgotten about them."

I admired them, and she said she'll be right back.

She came back with nothing on but the lingerie, and my eyes went wide.

"Like it?" she said, grinning flirtatiously.

I woke up besides Mags in the morning, with the light streaming in through the windows. I sighed in relief, being safe in the light.

Gosh. Last night sure was… something like never before. Getting chased by evil itself… and then I looked at still naked Mags, and I embarrassedly looked away from the riding crop that Mags was clutching in her hand as she slept.

I got off the bed to clothe myself, but she slapped my ass with the riding crop one last time.

I took a shower in her bathroom, then made her some breakfast, some breakfast sandwiches, sausage and eggs, and greeted her at the table as she was yawning and dressed in a shirt and underwear.

We ate the sandwiches, and kept on accidentally staring at each other too long.

She smiled as she looked into my eyes.

I tried making conversation, and said, "I think… I need to leave you-"

She frowned, and said, "That's a shitty way to break up with someone, Paul. Have awesome, kinky sex all night… make her breakfast… and not even let her finish her sandwich first. Shame on you! This is the best breakfast sandwich I've ever had!" waving her sandwich at me accusingly.

I smiled, and said, "Not that. I just need to die."

"…Oh. That took a turn… Um… Should I call the hospital?" she said.

I sighed, and said, "No… But- I think if I take the Devil with me… then Yule or someone can work on the others… and life will have a better chance…"

She held my hand, and said, "We have a better chance if you do too. Stay alive, stay with me, and we can figure this out together."

I squeezed her hand, and we talked about other things, politics and the like. Sports, economy, environment, crap like that. The environment was actually starting to get better, with everyone driving electric cars and finding alternatives to oil. Even the meat market was down, with the new veggie burgers being extremely popular in fast food. Mags just liked this local butcher's meat and eggs, who picked up all their products from local farms, a more common practice today. It would be a shame if all of that ended because of demons.

She took her shower, we talked some more, and Mags got dressed properly as we talked in her room. I noticed all the scratch marks on her back from my claws... but she actually enjoyed my claws and all the spiky parts of my body. She said making love with me was like opening a present with barbed wire ribbons.

Then we went to church.

We sat in the very back row, and usually listened to the normal priest drone on and on... but today there was a replacement priest, someone from the Middle East.

He started off his sermon with jokes. He used props and the like.

Everyone was laughing in this awesome sermon. I felt like I was listening to my best friend speak. He seemed like a cool guy, and somehow... when he spoke, you understood in a way that meant that he understood you.

I shook his hand vigorously after the mass. It felt like I shook some important person's hand... but I couldn't think of what that handshake reminded me of...

Mags smiled to him, and said as we walked past the priest out of the church, "I liked his account of Mary Magdalene, that even though she was in one of the lowest positions of society, possessed by demons as a prostitute, she still rose to be the first person to see Jesus after he rose from the dead. That priest... spoke of her like he knew her... If I didn't know any better, I'd say he was Jesus incognito."

I blinked for a second, stopped walking, and looked down at my hand that shook the priest's hand.

I had tried to talk to the priest again, but he seemed to have vanished.

Everyone said he had an important flight to catch.

I went home, and stared at the knives in my hands in my apartment.

I reminded myself of Tricia.

That time she played saxophone naked for me on the couch.

That time she nearly fell out the window, trying to help a wounded bird out of a tree.

That time we had a candlelit dinner, with her own cooking. The food... It probably was only good because it was such a nice little date. I had never had such... interesting spaghetti sauce. She made it herself. The garlic bread was burned to a crisp, but still... I think that was the best meal I ever had.

Then she died.

In a way, I enjoyed being around her memories. In a way, they were comforting.

But the longer I stayed in this solitude... the sadder I got. I sighed, and knew I needed to go outside.

I stood in the sunlight, just smoking a cigarette.

I finished the cigarette, and went back inside to my solitude.

Tricia was waiting on the sofa.

"Heya, Paul. How's the girlfriend and crap?" she said.

"G-Go away. I know you're not Tricia. I know you're some demon pulling a prank." I said.

Tricia laughed, and said, *"And you thought I was so pure... It is me, Tricia. Did you think I fucking fell for you because I liked you?? You're a piece of shit demon who should've remained dead. I was scared of you, Paul. You're a demon. And now I am too."*

"I know Tricia would never speak like that." I said.

"But you don't know about the guy who she fucked because she was bored. You don't know about the one she slept with just for fun. You don't know who he is... Well, I'll give you a hint. It starts with a ME!" the Devil said, and changed into a tall muscular man, with golden locks of hair and rippling biceps. The Devil continued, *"It happened in the summer... by a lake. She was alone, and I was stalking her. She thought I was soooo cool... and then the fun began. I even had her on her knees at one point! She was sucking like there was no-"*

"Forget it, Satan. I won't ever believe you." I said.

He grinned, and said, *"I don't need you to. I just need you to question the fact."*

I blinked, and he disappeared.

I decided not to live in Tricia's apartment anymore. For even though all her memories were here for me... They were here for someone else too, for him to defile.

30

I had already given most of Tricia's stuff back to her family, everything besides her knife.

I gave away everything else, and only went to Mags's with what clothes and other necessities I could fit in a backpack.

I invited Dylan to hang out with us, because besides him being such a good guy, I wanted to be around as many people as possible.

I didn't want to be alone for Satan to strike.

Mags invited some people from her work, and Dylan... well, he started volunteering at an animal shelter, and invited some people from there to come over too.

I invited Yule and Max.

Yule and Max were far older than *most* of us... besides the old lady who worked at the animal shelter that Dylan invited. Mags asked him why he invited her, and he said, "What? She's cool."

We had a little party.

I looked at all the people who had brought their friends, and friends of friends, all dancing, drinking, and laughing happily.

I tried to smile.

Mags said it looked like I had something stuck in my teeth.

I tried to pick it out, but she laughed and said, "Don't try too hard. You looked like instead of having happiness, you had to fart."

She kissed me, and I felt a bit happier after that.

The old lady was downing shots like nothing else, quicker than any of us young kids.

She looked me in the eyes as I scrutinized her, hoping she wasn't a demon.

She challenged me to a chess game.

I looked at her in surprise, and she laughed and brought out the board that Mags had. I hadn't played chess since I was a kid.

We played, and whenever she took one of my pieces, she took a shot of whiskey.

I soon only had a king, a queen, a rook, a bishop, and a knight, strangely enough. She went for every other piece first. My pawns fell like loyal soldiers, loyal soldiers to a ruthless warlord, her queen.

She said, "You let people pick at you too hard… You let them take everything, toy with you, play with you… You have all you need, with only a few."

I had been working up to this for a long while. I saw my opening.

I moved the queen by her king, with the other pieces defending the queen and blocking the escape route.

I said, "Checkmate."

"You have all you need… I was trying to weaken you, distract you with loss… but you have all you need with a few pieces. Congratulations. Next time… I won't be so drunk." the old lady said, and smiled.

I thought of her words, as she stumbled off to the bathroom.

I had my friends, I had my family. We could take Satan and his minions back to Hell, if we tried.

Yule and Max were dancing a couple's sort of dance, and everyone admired them as they turned and circled around with each other.

The party dwindled down to just Max, Yule, Dylan, Mags and I. We sat drinking in the kitchen, and I asked Yule how she defeated Satan before.

"It actually wasn't me. It was Sax who defeated Satan." she said.

I thought about it… It made sense. The demons did call Sax the usurper.

"He can't help us this time… But my father… I need to ask him a question." I said.

I went out to the porch with a cigarette, and called my father. My real father, Kasey. The man who's looked after me all my life.

He was glad to hear from me, said I was getting a little too secluded sometimes. I exchanged pleasantries, then grew grim, and asked him what I really wanted to ask.

I asked him how… how come he loved me like he did.

He just said, "You're my son, Paul."

"But I am from someone else. From someone who raped your wife. How can you not hate me? For what I even just represent?" I said.

He said, "Huh. I never thought of it like that. But I'd say you had no part to play in that act of violence. But maybe I love you because… because you come from a part of the woman I love. Maybe I just couldn't bear to leave a child to suffer, abandoned by his father. Maybe it's just fatherly instinct. Maybe.

"But I do know… I see a part of myself in you. You may not come from me directly, but you come from me spiritually.

"Maybe it's all the religion your mother is so fond of rubbing off on me… but I believe God loves all his children, even the most unwanted, and that I love you, Paul."

"…I love you too, Dad. I need to tell you- you and Mom- that I'm a demon-" I started.

But he said, "We know, Paul. We saw those scary parts of you since when they first started popping up. We were very worried for a long time. But maybe that's just bad genes… At least you can fly. I wouldn't worry about it if I was you."

I smiled, and said, "Love can see through any illusion. Goodnight, Dad."

"Goodnight, Paul. Remember to pray." my dad said, and we hung up.

I went back inside, and to my surprise my friends were all talking about how to help me… how to help me defeat Satan.

I talked with them a bit, and we devised a couple of plans. Then they followed me out the door to meet the Devil.

31

I went to the church in the night with Dylan, Mags, Yule and Max. It was unlocked.

"You really think you'll find the Devil *here?*" Mags said.

"No. But I know he'll find us here." I said, and shouted out to the empty church, "I challenge you, Satan. On your pride as the King of Hell. I challenge you to face me in this holy sanctuary… unless you're too scared to meet your maker."

A shadow that moved on its own crept through a stained glass window, and stopped before us.

Satan arose from the darkness.

Yule had her sword and flame ready for battle, I had my knives bared, and I told Dylan, Mags, and Max to step back. Dylan and Mags went behind the altar and pulpit. Max refused to step down, and raised his fists up to fight.

It was time for plan A. Kill Satan if we could.

We warily opposed him, and he laughed that evil, menacing, awful laugh.

He was suddenly shrouded in a huge, dark red flame… full, screaming souls. I could never hear them when they were only a spark in Satan's hand… but now they were terrifyingly loud.

Sobbing, moaning, screaming… and all of them sounded like they were suffering.

Satan just laughed.

"Yule. Max. We meet again. It's been so long. How are the kids?" Satan said.

Max yelled out in frustration, and said, "Just because all of our children… don't make it, doesn't mean we can't still try."

"Don't let him get under your skin, Max." Yule said.

"You should be ashamed of inviting me here, Saul… What would God say to the thief you've let in his home? Too bad God can't speak. He's weak, he's a disgrace to his creation…. He's pathetic. Like all of you." Satan said.

Without warning, Satan reached forth his flame and attacked us with it.

All three of us dodged those twisting arcing blasts, trying to get closer to him, trying to smite him down.

The flame nearly caught Max and I, but Yule raised forth her own flame and defended us from Satan's fires.

Her white, holy, pure flame blocked Satan's blazes. Wherever he would shoot at us, Yule swiped her own flame at it, cutting off the blast.

Frustrated, Satan pulled his pistol, and shot at… Mags.

Dylan pulled her out of the way just in time, and the bullet only went through Mags's arm instead of her heart.

Max tackled Satan to the ground. Satan instantly had the pistol pointed at Max's head, but Max used a self defense move and jammed the pistol away from him, disarming Satan himself.

Satan grinned, and breathed out fire on Max.

Max had barely any time to push himself away, and his shirt was on fire from the blast. He quickly tore it off and tried to stamp out the fire.

The fire wouldn't go out. It set fire to the floor, it kept on spreading, growing remarkably quick.

Yule grabbed Max as he was coughing from the smoke, and led the others out of the church.

Satan tried to follow them, but I blocked his path.

I turned to Mags one last time, as she was clutching her arm, and nodded to her. I think she understood. I could almost feel her praying for me.

I turned back to Satan, this evil, awful monstrosity. He looked exactly like a demon now, nothing beautiful about him.

His golden wings were shredded, his malevolent face in ugly fury.

I looked into his eyes... and I saw all the flames of Hell contained in them.

"I think this belongs to you." I said, and threw him my knife. He looked at it, as the flames were engulfing the church.

The flames actually didn't feel so bad to me. Felt kind of comfy. They licked up and down my arm, not burning me.

Satan picked up the blade, and said, *And the other?*

"That belongs to Tricia." I said.

Satan wielded his knife like a murderer... like Cain killing Abel.

I wielded Tricia's like an eternal gladiator.

We circled each other in the flames.

Satan gnashed his teeth and roared.

I was silent.

We both struck at each other, dancing back and forth in fire. He went for my neck, for my gut, slashing and stabbing wildly.

I was sweating as the fires of Hell reached out for me with that blade.

He stabbed at my heart, and in a move of great expertise... a move a great warrior once taught me, Felix himself, my first and only trainer...

I deflected the blade with my dagger, and lunged at Satan.

I was getting closer and closer, about to stab Satan in the throat.

But someone pulled me back. The bull man, Molech.

Darcy the succubus slashed at me with her claws, cutting open my skin through my clothes.

All the demons of creation were in this church, together defending their master.

They held me down to my knees, endless rats, demonic minions, ugly, awful things.

Satan raised his blade, about to execute me. There was no way out. I knew I would die.

So I delayed the inevitable.

And worked on plan B.

A last bet… one more Hail Mary should do it…

"You can't even fight by yourself… What cowardice…" I said.

Satan faltered before he was about to cut off my head with the dagger, and said, *"I am not so prideful as to not accept every opportunity. You are a fool, Saul. You even gave me one of your weapons."*

"I just wanted to send you back to Hell with all the baggage you brought. And it's Paul." I said.

Molech mooed, and Darcy hissed at me.

The other demons all cackled, snickered, and roared.

"I own this world, as I will own your soul." Satan said, about to slice again.

I said, "You are trapped in this world, like me. As you are trapped in this church. There is no way out. I made extra sure to ask the man upstairs for a favor… I prayed my heart out, over and over… and I think he heard me."

"What did you pray for?" Satan said, and laughed, *"A quick end to your suffering?"*

"I prayed for him to take me to Hell."

As I finished my Hail Mary, the roof collapsed, the burning building's foundations broke, and fell on all of us.

The ground seemed to open up, and we were taken back to Hell.

"NO! NO! NO!" Satan roared, as all the demons that were in creation fell to the lowest pits of Hell.

I smiled as I hit every ledge in Hell, feeling like I was dying over and over. At least Satan and his minions were too. Our knives fell back into the pit from whence they came.

Someone grabbed onto my hand from a ledge, and someone grabbed onto my foot from below.

I looked up, and Sax was holding my hand and smiling at me, a human again.

I looked down, and Satan was holding onto my foot, furiously glaring at me.

"If you go back, then I do too!" Satan said.

"Hm?" Sax said, "We're not going back to the living world. C'mon, you two." and he helped us up onto the ledge.

I followed Sax, as Satan did as well, into Purgatory.

Part 7: Gula

Gluttony

32

———

I asked Sax, "Uh.. I thought you went to Heaven?"

Sax laughed, and said, "I did! I'm just doing some volunteer work. They always need a few souls helping the lost and confused through Purgatory, and I thought it would be a great way to spend my eternal time."

"So… You really amended every mistake? You really feel bad for what you did?" I said.

He looked at me sadly as we were walking through the park, and said, "More than I ever did. But I still feel like I need to do more. They argued with me over and over… saying I did enough… Eventually, they made the case that someone who keeps saying they want to truthfully keep amending their sins probably has amended enough… So they accepted me into Heaven, and I made them put me in Purgatory part time. It was the least I could do. Heaven's boring anyway, and I prefer spending my time with purpose."

Satan was creeping around behind the trees and bushes. He snarled at me when I turned to look at him.

But he still followed us through Purgatory.

I whispered to Sax, "Are you sure you want *him* to come with us?"

"Oh yes. I believe he's got a bit to amend." Sax said.

So we stopped at a garden in Purgatory, a nice place... filled with all sorts of animals, all peacefully enjoying each other's company.

Sax took out a list, cleared his throat, and said, "One of your first sins, Paul. Stealing those apples from that farmer and not paying for it. You must plant a tree for every apple you stole."

"Ok... Doesn't seem so hard. I only took seven of them." I said, and got to work, picking up a shovel nearby and planting the saplings that were laying in a pile.

Sax turned his head to Satan, who was watching me. Sax said, "And you know what you did here, don't you, Satan."

I looked at Satan snickering, and I saw a man and a woman watching him as well.

They were unclothed, but they still hid their shame.

"It was their own gluttony that got them out of the garden. I only gave them a suggestion." Satan said.

"Say sorry." the naked woman said to Satan.

Satan just laughed, and said, *"I'd rather do this."*

And Satan ripped out the sapling I had just planted, and snapped it in half.

I looked at him angrily for a second, sighed, and kept working on the saplings.

Satan took a bunch of apples from low hanging branches in the garden, and gorged himself on the fruit.

Smack, smack, smack. I heard him smacking on the apples as I worked.

He threw an apple core at the back of my head. I just kept working.

He sang some annoying, insulting song about my mother... and I just tried to focus on the work, no matter how much he aggravated me.

Eventually, I looked happily at the apple trees planted by me. In a way, as I remembered the taste of those stolen apples I ate, they seemed to taste sweeter in my memory, after the guilt was finally gone.

The man and woman thanked me for helping them in their garden. And Satan hissed at them like a snake, and we kept walking through Purgatory.

We found a man sitting under a tree and admiring nature. He had only one arm, and waved to me with his left.

I put my fists up, ready to destroy this man... Ready to make him suffer for the pain and death he inflicted on Tricia.

But Sax said, "Woah now, Paul... Terence just wants to make ammends to *you.* You did nothing wrong when you and him fought each other in life... You were both played like a fiddle by Georgia."

The boxer, Georgia's husband, Terence, came up to me, and offered his left hand to shake. He said, "I think I will be here for a lot longer than you... and still, with only one arm. I'm sorry."

I said, not shaking his hand, "How can I ever forgive you. *You* threatened to kill me and attacked me because your wife told you to, your wife who raped me. *You* were the one who told the demons to kill me quickly in your basement. *You* murdered Tricia Antonelli."

He put down his hand, and said, "I know. I thought so many awful things... but I really did believe I loved Georgia, even though I felt like I was in Hell with her. She was- She was my greatest achievement, and I felt like my life was meaningless without her... and she took everything I had away..."

I crossed my arms, and said, "It's your own damn fault. Don't blame your actions on Georgia."

He looked at his feet, and said, "I know... I saw her for what she was, very briefly... I was never so scared of a woman, a woman that I loved, when I was beside her in Hell..."

"So you saw that she was a demon after you died. Good for you." I said.

"No. I mean when I was alive. After she made me be so… tortured. I thought I was doing it for love… but maybe I was just frightened, or maybe I was really just clinging onto hate." he said, "Will you please, if you won't forgive me, then find some way for me to make restitution for my evil? Take my other arm, if it will please you."

"I don't want your arms. I want Tricia back." I said.

He sighed, and said, "I thought you would say that. I said the same thing when talking about Georgia."

I frowned. I said, "Why… Why did you love her?"

He shrugged, and said, "I wanted her. And only her. I can't say it was real love… but I believed it was."

Satan laughed awfully at him, at both of us. Satan said, *"She always did say you were inadequate in bed… after I was done fucking her."*

Terence frowned at Satan, and said, "If I only knew you weren't her brother, and were really the Prince of Darkness… I could've stopped you."

Satan said, *"Cry about it some more. I'm sure that'll get you somewhere nice and pretty like Paradise."*

"Leave him alone, Satan." I said. I turned back to Terence and said, "We were both victims, I guess. I wish our paths never crossed, and we didn't have to inflict so much suffering on each other."

"Thank you. I still need to admire nature some more, as I never fully appreciated it as much as I could've. Would you care to join me?" Terence said.

I shrugged, and we sat by the tree, watching the ants climb up and down the trunk.

We sat for a long time like that, just watching ants. I guess we're all sort of ants to God, all connected in our own little world… but still, these ants made the tree flourish and prosper, they took care of it, despite one ant only being one ant.

Satan was tapping his foot, waiting for us to be done, but Sax let us watch the ants.

And we both got up after sitting in silence for so long, and I said, "Take care of yourself, Terence."

He said, "You too. You'll see Tricia again in Heaven… I may see Georgia again in Hell. Pray for me, tell God to not let me go back."

"I will. Just watch nature instead. She's a far greater mistress than any demon from Hell." I said.

He nodded, and I shook his left hand.

33

We took a break by a bench, and Sax noticed the little package on it and exclaimed in delight. "Biscottis! That Angelica Nestor… She knows just what I need to brighten up my day." Sax offered me the whole bag, and I took only one biscotti. Sax crunched on the rest of the biscottis happily.

Satan looked on enviously, greedily, gluttonously. Sax offered him a biscotti, and Satan grabbed the whole thing and devoured them as quickly as he could.

Sax shrugged, and said, "You must like biscottis even more than me!" Satan tried to wipe the crumbs off his face.

We kept walking, and it was a peaceful park. In the end I noticed that I kept passing the same tree over and over, one with a notched marking on it… I looked closer at the marking, and it was a heart with "Tricia and Paul" in the center. I had done that before to this tree in high school.

I put my hand on the tree, and felt the notch. I felt all my old high school memories… things I could've done but didn't, people I could've helped, but turned my back on… people who mattered, but I forgot.

I felt saddened by this tree, by this mark. The only good thing that I kept from high school was my relationships with a few friends. I wish I knew what I knew now then.

I kept on walking down the path, but didn't see the tree anymore. Sax was humming along, enjoying the walk. Satan was lagging and panting behind us. *"How much longer to Heaven? I'm going to destroy them all when we get there, you know."* Satan said.

"With that attitude, you'll never get there! We're nearly at the next stop." Sax said.

We got a large mountain, and Satan groaned looking upwards at it.

"That's the upwards path to Heaven! We've got so many sins to get through… but some important people want to meet you, Paul, so I'm sure they'll be lenient and you can get around to it later. Up we go!" Sax said.

My wings felt so heavy… like they were lead on my back. I laboriously hiked instead. We went trudging up the mountain. Sax seemed to be enjoying the walk, and as I looked at him whistling and hiking, I started to enjoy it too. The view was like nothing else, seeing all across… the afterlife, from the mountainside. Hell was a large pit on the horizon, and when I looked upwards to those clouds… I felt like Heaven was so close, even though it would be a long, long time to go.

Satan was gasping for breath as we trudged up the mountainside, then sat down and said, *"Forget it. I'll go back down if this is so hard."*

"You'd really give up Heaven… again??" Sax said. Satan seemed to ponder at that, and grumbled. "I'll give you a lift… I guess… Everyone deserves a chance…" Sax said, and sighed, and was about to give Satan a piggyback ride.

But I said, "No. Let him stay. Fuck this evil thing. Let him go back to Hell if he desires."

The mountainside collapsed, and we fell in an avalanche. I bounced and rolled down the mountain, and soon… we were back to where we started.

I groaned as I looked back up the mountainside.

"Oh well... Let's just try again. We've got another chance." Sax said.

Satan grumbled, and sat.

I guess he deserved a chance... I guess... Through everything he did to me, there was no one I'd rather turn my back on... but... I suppose it didn't matter in the end...

So I offered Satan my back, and he hopped on. I carried him up the mountainside.

Satan was a heavy bastard, and every step I took was a step for two.

We kept on going, stopping for rests occasionally, and climbed up the mountain.

I just thought of my old life... everything I did... Did it matter? I suppose life is just an experience after all. I was happy to have lived it.

We were at the peak, after what felt like days in Purgatory... We were at the peak of the mountain.

But instead of what I expected, the gates of Heaven, there was a stage set up for us, with a guitar, drums, and a bass on the stage, ready to be played. Sax sat in the seats, and smiled as he looked at me. I thought that was odd.

I inspected the stage, as Satan swore at God for being such a tease, and it was a fantastically, almost heavenly looking stage. It seemed familiar though, like every good thing of my past.

I walked on the stage, like I had done before in life.

I knew someone was watching me. Watching everyone, always, there for you no matter what.

I gulped as I felt that feeling.

I saw someone descend from the clouds, a beautiful, majestic angel, with gorgeous white wings. I gasped as she got closer and heavenly... saxophones, heralded her approach.

Tricia said, "Hey Paul."

She immediately hugged me, and I was so flabbergasted it took me a second to hug her back.

"Tricia!! I- I never thought I'd see you again!!" I said.

"I knew I'd see you. I had faith." she said, and smiled.

I just hugged her forever… I felt like I never needed to go to Heaven, if Tricia was here with me.

But she said, "It's the final show for us. It's time to see if we've got the stuff. Ready?"

"…Huh? For what?" I said.

"For the final test to get into Heaven, duh! God wants to see if you truly learned something from your life, if it truly had value to you. I suggested that we put on a show for him, since music seemed to be the one thing that gave your life true meaning." Tricia said, and smiled.

"Wh-What? I have to play for God? You've… *talked* to God??" I said.

"Yeah, so? I thought it was about time. Dude was so pissed for me… y'know, me dying because of Satan's scheme, but you know God… He always forgives. He's letting Satan play with us three." she said.

"Us three?" I said.

"You know the veils between the living and the dead can be thin at times. Some people pass into the afterlife just with a dream." Tricia said, and smiled, "I think Mags would love to see you again."

"…Oh. I'm sorry for what happened between me and her. But we truly did care for each other, and being with each other made us not feel so bad about losing you." I said.

"It's alright. What else would you do if your lover was dead? I'm honestly happier you fucked Mags instead of kill yourself. That would've been *such* a bummer. Plus, I think some good came out of it." Tricia said.

"…What do you mean?" I asked.

But Mags walked out from behind the stage, yawned, and said, "Gosh my lucid dreams are getting weirder… Whatever. Might as well make it a wet one. Paul! Tricia! Take off your clothes!"

I laughed, and gave her a hug. She slowly hugged me back.

She said to me, "I wanted to say something to you Paul... I- I never got to-"

"It's alright. I feel like you were one of my best friends, too." I said.

"Not that. It's just-" she said.

I just kept squeezing her tight, and she squeezed me back.

"I'm pregnant, you dream dope." she said.

I stared at her. She was telling the truth. "It won't be like me, will it?" I said.

"I sure hope not. I'd hate to have to file the kid's spiky parts down every day..." Mags said.

"Ok... I... wish I was there for you." I said.

"It's alright. I mean, it's not, you're dead, but at least I have something to remember you by..." Mags said.

"Alright. Let's play for God." I said.

"I've missed playing with you deadies... I'm going to feel so sad when I wake up..." Mags said, but got behind the drum set as Tricia picked up the bass.

I turned to the Beast, and said, "Are you ready, Satan?"

"I'm not playing with you, not on your soul." Satan said.

"Oh well. You weren't half bad at guitar, Paul. Let's do this!" Tricia said.

But Satan ran to the guitar... raised it over his head... and smashed it on the stage.

"Why did you do that?!" I yelled.

Satan grinned, and said, *"However will you play now... I know how... I've got a guitar. Why not use that?"*

A demonic instrument appeared in his hands, red as blood, a satanic axe.

"...What do you want for it?" I asked.

"Your soul. I want you to come back to Hell. If you don't take it... I will be eternally tormenting your child... forever. Just as I did to you. Take it... Please God with this guitar, finish your song... and he... and I... will be merciful on your spawn." Satan said.

I growled at him.

But I accepted the guitar.

I did not want my child to suffer through my original sin, and even if I must give up my chance at Paradise, I will do this.

We got ready to play, with Sax and Satan watching in the stands, and God watching from… everywhere.

I strummed the notes, playing a song I had been practicing in my head for a while now. Mags started the beat, and Tricia played bass.

I sang, "I'll be back, my love, in a thousand years,

"I'll be back, and I'll wipe off the tears.

"I'll be there, my love, for you as well.

"I'll be here, my love, for you in Hell."

I played the guitar.

It felt so heavy after a bit… it felt like every string was painful on my fingertips…

I couldn't keep going. And I dropped the guitar.

Mags and Tricia tried to keep going, but I could not pick up the guitar. It hurt me to even approach it.

I didn't know what to do. I thought I would fail. I thought I would suffer through Hell forever… as my children would… and my children's children… on and on and over and over…

But someone came out from the back.

My first guitarist, Renley, and he picked up the guitar.

"I'll always be by your side, Paul. You're my best mortal enemy… my friend." he said, and continued the notes as I sang.

I sang, "I'm going to Heaven, through Purgatory's grace.

"I'm coming for you, to be back in this place.

"I love you, my love, for a thousand years.

"And an eternity more, I'll wipe off the tears."

Soon the pain was too much for Renley as well, and he dropped it.

But my sister, Dana, came out from the back, and picked up the guitar. She said, "You'll always be my brother. No matter who you may be from originally."

And she played with us.

I sang, "To the end we will be, in the tears like sea.

"I wash them away, with the love we will be.

"We'll end the torment, and be one again.

"We'll be together my love, even after the end."

But she dropped it as well.

My last guitarist, Dylan, came out from the back, and played as long as he could. He said, "It's really not so bad being honest if you can. Thanks for giving me a chance at my soul again when you stole it."

I sang, "The fears are gone, our friends are here.

"There's nothing else, but to have another beer.

"To laugh and smoke, and be together again.

"I've washed off the tears, and we're-"

But he also dropped the guitar. There was no one else.

I tried to sing, but I couldn't think of the words.

Satan was grinning at me, and I felt like I was disappointing even God.

But someone else came out from the back, and picked up the guitar. The person whose guitar I first tried to play. The man whose cared for me all my life, even though he had no biological reason to.

My father, Kasey.

He played it the longest out of all of us. He kept going at the guitar as it bled his fingertips, as it burst to flame in his hands, he would not let it go.

I sang, "We're together in Heaven."

We finished the song for God.

Sax clapped loudly, and Satan stood up in rage.

"So be it. Your father saved his son... But you will never be able to save yours. I will come for your CHILDREN!! Every child of Adam and Eve are mine for their sins!" Satan said.

My father, Kasey, said, "Ever heard of baptism, Satan? We have amended the sins of our parents... Every one of them. Now go back to Hell, and take your sins with you."

Sax, my genetic father, said, "He can't go back yet! There's so much sins he has to amend! See, look at all the people climbing up the mountain! They're so close to Paradise... but they all want to talk to you... Satan."

Satan turned his head at the crowd coming over the mountainside pass. They were all angrily glaring at Satan.

Stairs came from the sky, a glorious stairway to Heaven, and Tricia said, "C'mon, Paul."

"Really? Right now? But..." I said.

"The Lord has heard, and He has answered." she said, offering me a hand to take.

I looked to her, then to Mags and my guitarists all waiting happily.

I rushed to my band, and gave them all a hug, or a kiss in Mag's case, and hugged my father, my real father, the longest out of all of them. He said to me, "We'll miss you, Paul."

Mags said, "What should I name our child?"

"Whatever you like. I'll always be watching out for you and the child. Let him know... his father cares." I said.

She burst out crying, and gave me a hug again, squeezing me tight.

They all woke up, disappearing from Purgatory.

Satan was trying to push his way past the crowd that enveloped him, all demanding that he make restitutions for his evil. He watched in anger as I took Tricia's hand, and I ascended the stairs.

Sax said, "Goodbye, Paul! Have a good afterlife!" and waved to me.

I smiled and waved back at him, and we got to the gates of Heaven. I said hello to St. Peter again, and he opened the gates for me.

I'd describe all the fantastic things in Heaven, but what would be the point of that? You'll see it for yourself when you get there.

Epilogue

That is the story of Paul. It's really not a happy ending if you think about it.

A young man died because he sacrificed himself to protect the world from horrible evil. Does that remind you of anyone?

Anyway, I prayed for Paul every day, like I did for everyone I knew. I watched his child grow up, despite unable to have one of my own. Max and I tried over and over again… but it could be something with my biology. It is my one regret that I cannot pass on my life… but, since I already have an extra life, I suppose I'm doing that anyway.

Maggie cares for the kid like nothing else. She's a great mother, and even though she keeps on having trysts with random people… she only does so because she hopes one of them can be a father or second mother to her child.

Dana and Dylan got together, since Dana couldn't ever find that perfect love, so thought she'd settle for someone who at least was completely different from her original ideals for a perfect love. Eventually though… she thought Dylan was *too* perfect, so they broke up. Now Dana spends a lot of time with Maggie, and helps raise her child in her off times.

Satan *tried* to amend his mistakes… but because he has committed so many sins, he'll probably be in Purgatory forever, for God's sake. But what can I say? The promise of Paradise is fantastically rich.

I continued my role as an angel on Earth, but I knew that the world was safe now, because of a man named Paul.

Mags sang a song for Paul at the end of the funeral.

"I'll be back, my love, in a thousand years,
I'll be back, and I'll wipe off the tears.
I'll be there, my love, for you as well.
I'll be here, my love, for you in Hell.
I'm going to Heaven, through Purgatory's grace.
I'm coming for you, to be back in this place.
I love you, my love, for a thousand years.
And an eternity more, I'll wipe off the tears.
To the end we will be, in the tears like sea.
I wash them away, with the love we will be.
We'll end the torment, and be one again.
We'll be together my love, even after the end.
The fears are gone, our friends are here.
There's nothing else, but to have another beer.
To laugh and smoke, and be together again.
I've washed off the tears, and we're together in Heaven."